CANNIBAL
PLATEAU

George Noon or "California"
Shannon

CANNIBAL PLATEAU

A Novel

Joe Wise

SUNSTONE
PRESS

SANTA FE

For my parents
who took me to the mountains

Sunstone books may be purchased for educational, business, or sales promotional use. For information please write: Special Markets Department, Sunstone Press, P.O. Box 2321, Santa Fe, New Mexico 87504-2321.

Library of Congress Cataloging-in-Publication Data:

Wise, Joe, 1939–
    Cannibal plateau: a novel / by Joe Wise.—1st ed.
        p. cm.
    ISBN: 0-86534-262-8—ISBN: 0-86534-360-8 (pbk.)
    I. Title.
    PS3573 . 1787. 1787C36   1997
    813' .54—dc21   97-9369
                                       CIP

Published in

SUNSTONE PRESS
Post Office Box 2321
Santa Fe, NM 87504-2321 / USA
(505) 988-4418 / *orders only* (800) 243-5644
FAX (505) 988-1025
www.sunstonepress.com

Cover art: Drawing from a sketch by John A. Randolph.
Harper's Weekly, October 17, 1874.

PREFACE

A COLORADO TRAGEDY

On the 17th of November, 1873, a party
of twenty-one miners left Salt Lake City for the
San Juan Mines, in Colorado, taking a short
route by the old Gunnison trail across the
mountains. . . . The party arrived at the Ute
encampment, at the junction of the
Uncompahgre and Gunnison rivers, on January 20, 1874. OURAY, chief of the Utes, advised the party not to proceed across the
mountains, as it was very dangerous at that
time of year on account of the snow, but to
remain at his camp until spring, when the
route would be open. . . . On the 9th of February a party of six, (lead by "AL" PACKER), left
the Indian camp for the Los Pinos agency,
which they were informed was about seventy-
five miles distant. They had ten days' provisions. . . PACKER arrived at the agency alone
having been out sixty-five days. . . .The fate of
the missing men remained a mystery for several months, until the accidental discovery of
the camp where the bodies were lying. MR.
JOHN A. RANDOLPH, an artist, who was out
on a sketching tour in the Uncompahgre
Mountains, was startled one afternoon by
coming suddenly upon the remains of five human beings in a gloomy, secluded spot,
densely shaded by tall trees, at the foot of a
steep bluff near the bank of the Gunnison
River. Marks of violence on each body indicated
that a most terrible crime had been committed here.

—Harpers Weekly, October 17, 1874

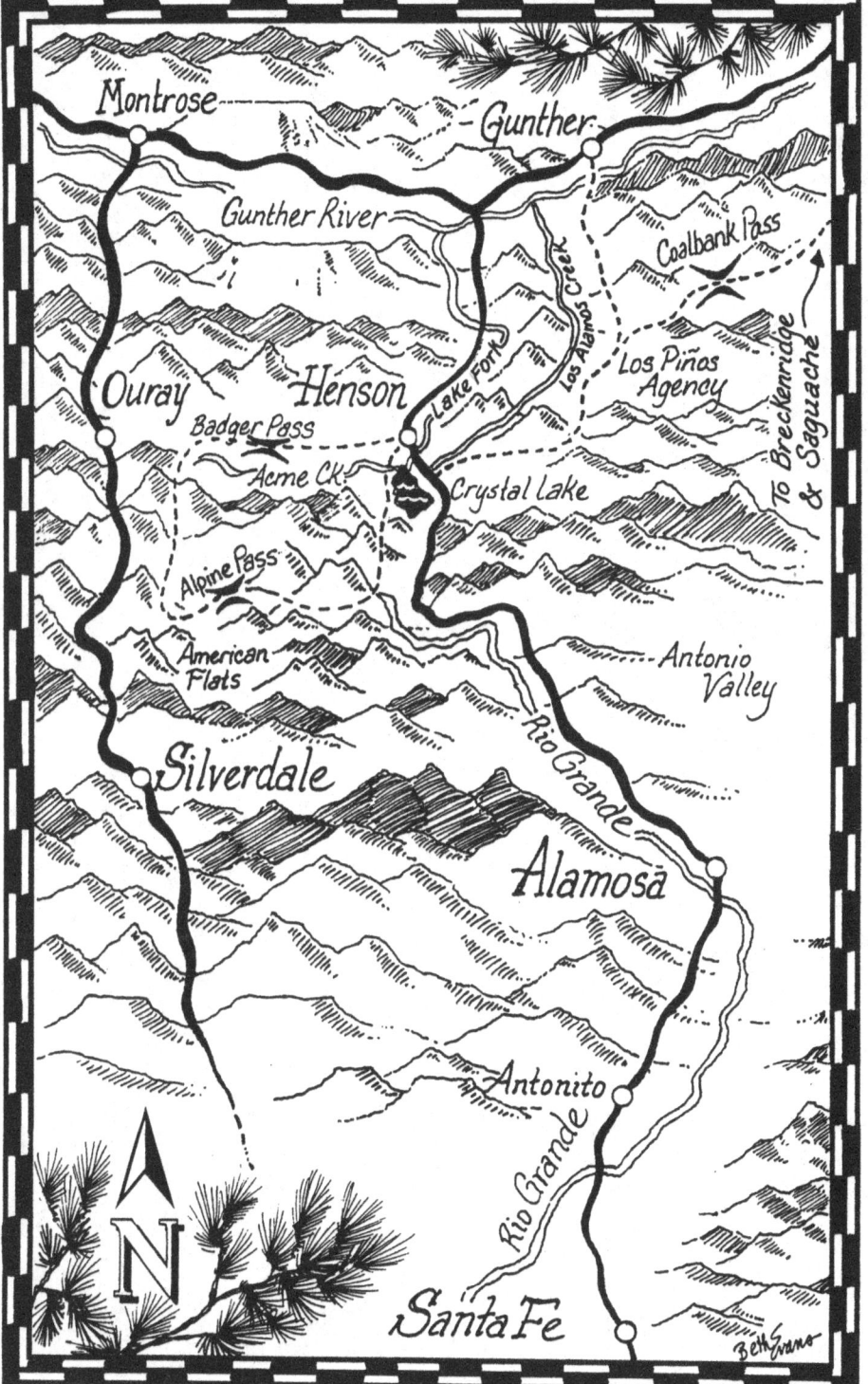

1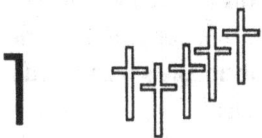

From where he sat in the rocks the gunman could see thirty yards of the narrow shelf-road below him. There the steep single-track strip cut into the canyon wall and turned sharply around a large rock outcropping. Lomax would be driving right at him, slowing the jeep to avoid the abrupt drop off. He would be visible for fifteen seconds. That's all he would need.

He shifted his crouched weight and steadied the rifle on a rock in front of him. Through the telescopic sight he could count the petals on flowers growing beside the road. Lomax had driven up to the mine an hour before and by now would have found what he was looking for and be headed back down the canyon. Any minute he would round the corner. With the open jeep angling down the steep incline, the windshield would be no obstacle. It would be easy.

He didn't hear the jeep at first. There was no wind but in the thin air of the high altitude the sound of the engine didn't carry well. However, he had been watching intently and saw the red fender when it first appeared, rolling slowly directly toward him. Through the scope he took a quick look at the license plate. It was Lomax's. He raised the rifle slightly and Lomax's face filled the scope, cross hairs centered on the bridge of his nose. Ten more seconds and he would turn.

The gunman didn't see the bullet strike and he couldn't see the pink spray that flew from the back of Lomax's head, but he looked up in time to see the jeep swerve sharply to the left, lurch forward and plunge over the unguarded road bank.

Its motor roaring as if it too were mortally wounded, the four-by-four hung suspended for an instant over the empty gorge sustained by its own noisy will, then failing, slowly nosed in a sickening arc, accelerating as it fell. Fifty feet down it struck the first ledge squarely with the unmistakable sound of smashed metal and glass, then flipped over, bouncing and careening end over end further down the rocky talus slope and out of sight.

The gunman worked the bolt of the rifle and ejected the spent cartridge onto the ground, picked it up and put it in his pocket. He broke the rifle down, wrapped the barrel and the sight and the stock separately in newspapers and put them in his bulky backpack. Then he laboriously shouldered it and began to work his way carefully down through the rocks.

It took more than an hour to reach the wreckage which lay wedged between two large boulders. Lomax's broken, lifeless body hung from the seat belt harness.

The gunman carefully pulled a two-gallon can from his backpack, opened it and poured gasoline over the jeep, saturating the seats, the floor mat and Lomax's limp body. As he turned to put the empty can back in the pack, the metal top fell onto the rocks. He heard it land, and looked unsuccessfully for it. Hurriedly, he unscrewed the cap from the jeep's fuel tank, made a roll of newspaper and stuffed in into the opening for a wick.

He backed away and crouched behind a stony outcropping. Wrapping a small rock in another piece of newspaper, he lit it with a match and tossed the burning missile toward the jeep. It fell short and bounced away. On the second try, the fire landed in the back seat and there was a blinding flash of light and a throaty WHARUMPF as the vehicle burst into flame.

Even behind the rocks he could feel the intense heat. It would boil Lomax's brain, exploding the skull leaving no clue about the gunshot wound. The flames would do the rest. Unfortunate accident.

He swung the backpack, lighter now, over his shoulder and satisfying himself with a final look, turned and started up the rocky gorge. He knew that soon black smoke from the burning tires would be visible for miles, but he had some time. It would be an hour or more before anyone would come up the road looking for the fire. By that time, he would be over the ridge where he had left the truck.

2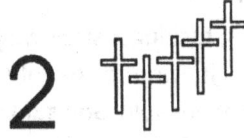

There is barely room enough in the narrow river valley for the painted buildings of the little wooden town. At its widest point from the eroded breccia cliffs along the river to the talus slope behind Bluff Street, Henson's neat rectangular grid work is only five blocks wide. A walker, who doesn't stop to talk, could travel its length from the Acme Creek bridge to the AMOCO station in less than five minutes and from the car-seat bench by the station office door could see the city limit signs at both ends of town.

For those who are preoccupied with the past, for those who, for whatever romantic personal reasons, yearn to see things as they might have been, for those who need to nurture in themselves the notion that it is possible to reach across time, Henson is as welcome a discovery as a potsherd or a pithouse.

Stranded in its rocky slip by a receding tide of fortune, the durable little mining town has not so much been preserved as spared. To be sure, many things have changed about Henson since its heyday as the Queen City of the San Juans. The dirt streets have been paved, running water and indoor plumbing have replaced the wash basin and the thunder jug, and trucks now deliver supplies that once arrived, accompanied by the metallic music of trace chains, in heavily loaded teamsters' wagons.

But the same cottonwoods still shade the same chinked log cabins and the same porched Victorian houses and arch, upper branches almost touching, over those same wide streets. Shoppers, now in Jeeps and Chevy suburbans, find what they need in the same five painted false-fronts on the single row of businesses across from the park and in the evenings, after dark, stars still dangle just out of reach and the air is still fragrant with the smoky incense of wood-and-coal stoves.

"Hello, Mary," David said as he entered the shop. Mary Hinsdale was sitting as usual in the back corner of her little shop, boxed within the familiar security of the cozy compartment formed by the right angle arrangement of two wood-and-glass showcases. She had looked up from her book when she heard the flat, metallic tinkle of the bell on the door.

"Hello, David," she said over half-glasses, tucking a stray wisp of gray hair behind her ear. Mary had owned the Alpine Gift Shop for twenty years. It was the only place in Henson County where books were sold. She said she only sold the gifts so she could afford to sell the books. Crowded around her on the counter tops near the cash register were stacks of catalogs, opened packs of cigarettes, an ash tray, a coffee pot and a blue and white china cup. Without getting off the stool, she could reach everything.

"How is it selling?" David asked, making his way carefully through the crowded shop. Mary knew he was referring to his book on Hawthorne's Fourth Expedition that had been published by the Colorado Historical Society earlier that summer.

"Eleven copies so far this week," Mary said, lowering her glasses and letting them hang from the cord around her neck.

"Well, it's a start," David said. He took a copy from the shelf and stood admiring the cover obviously pleased and still somewhat surprised that something he had written was for sale in the same shop where he had come for so many years to buy the books of others.

"Nice feeling, isn't it?" she said. "And it's a nice book," she added, smiling.

David was flattered and he nodded politely to acknowledge her compliment. He didn't actually know Mary well, only through the bookstore, but books had made them friends.

"I still have quite a few at the house if you need any more," David said gesturing with the book.

"You never know," Mary said. "There has certainly been quite a lot of interest. No one really knew much about the Hawthorne Expedition, even though it was only about fifty miles from here that they were lost. I guess the Hammit Massacre gets all the attention around here."

The Hammit Massacre was the local legend in Henson and it had been since that day in 1874 when the five butchered and rotting bodies were found. Alfred Hammit, an epileptic drifter and sole survivor of the prospecting party, had been convicted of murder and cannibalism. The grave site just above town at the foot of Cannibal Plateau, named after the event, was a regular stop for summer tourists.

"Do you and Dr. Fuller have anything else in mind for us?" she asked. "Another book?" She had been urging David to write a history of Henson and she never saw him without mentioning it. David had met Jack Fuller shortly after moving to Henson. They had worked together on the Hawthorne book and during that discovered they were good friends. People in town rarely saw one without the other.

"Well," David smiled, "writing the book was fun and I have to say it was all over much sooner than I expected. I thought researching that project would keep me busy for years. At least, that's what I had planned on." He and Mary had talked before about how long he had been interested in the Hawthorne Expedition and how, when the book had been published, he had felt a letdown now that the anticipation was over.

"Well, I'm sure you will think of something," she said fondly.

David put the book back in the shelf with the other copies and stood for a minute looking at it. He liked seeing his name on the cover.

There was no wasted space in the tiny shop. Rows of tiered wooden shelves lined the walls and covered most of the floor leaving only two narrow isles between them. David moved slowly between the shelves crowded with ceramic animals, cedar boxes and placards, salt-and-pepper shakers, baskets of perfumed soaps and candles. There were macrame plant hangers, painted tiles, pot holders, pencils made of aspen sticks, wood carvings, animal skins, framed photographs of mountain scenes and rectangular boxes of rock collections mounted like samplers of petrified candies. Woven baskets hung from nails near the ceiling. In the windows on either side of the door there were picture calendars and date books and boxes of assorted rocks—pyrite nuggets, Apache tears, petrified wood, quartz crystals and droplets of polished agate.

David glanced up to see his face reflected in a mirror on a shelf by the door. Somehow it wasn't the face he expected to see and for a moment he was taken by surprise. He brushed the hair back from his forehead. It was longer than he remembered and there were feathered wisps of gray in front of his ears.

The face that studied him from between the shelves was still angular and trim, cheek bones still prominent enough, the jaw line still well defined. But across the forehead and between the eyes just over the nosepiece of the glasses, someone had penciled thin, dark lines, and traced, from either side of the nose, a pair of broad lines, brackets, that curved downward toward the chin setting off the mouth's spare camber like a painted, parenthetical arc.

At fifty-four, David was the same age his father had been that first summer day they came into the shop looking for a present for his mother. But David didn't feel fifty-four. And the face in the mirror didn't look fifty-four, not the way fathers look fifty-four. Fathers had round, jowly faces and slicked back gray hair parted in the middle and bridgework in their smiles. The face in the mirror wasn't a fifty-four year old father's face. It was the face of a boy made up to look like a man.

David picked up a piece of ore the size of a baseball. The milky quartz veins were flecked with lead and silver and copper and bright yellow pieces of fool's gold. A piece of green felt had been glued to the rock's flat bottom. He hefted the rock in his hand and, smiling, took it with him as he walked to the counter.

"I could never resist these," he said, putting the rock down on the counter top.

"Makes a nice paper weight, "she replied, putting on her glasses to inspect it closely. "It's ore from the Golden Fleece mine."

"O-o-o," David worried aloud. "This won't bring bad luck to me too, will it?"

"Oh, no," Mary reassured him. "The curse only falls on the owner of the mine. This little piece of ore won't hurt you. And you'll be able to make use of it, won't you," she said, smiling playfully as she handed him the bag. "You can use it to keep the breeze from blowing away the pages of your new manuscript."

David shook his head in mock exasperation. "Thanks," he said. "Good idea."

The bell tinkled again as David left. Outside, there was no one on the shadowed boardwalk connecting the five false-front stores that made up what was left of the town's Victorian business district. The bank had closed at three o'clock. In a few minutes Mary would close the gift shop. There was one car in front of the grocery store. It was a quiet afternoon. The tourists and the fishermen would not come until after the fourth of July.

The thin mountain air was light and cool and the extra flannel shirt felt good. He stood for a moment memorizing the pleasant, easy rhyme of the afternoon. Across the street, the park was empty except for one bench near the swings where three identical old men sat facing the sun, napping in what was left of the day like gray birds turned to the wind. Beyond the park, close across the quiet comfort of the valley, beyond the weathered, wooden order of the little town, beyond the line of pointed river trees, the oversized mountains, their pastels fully sun-lit, stood shoulder to shoulder in a protective arc against the sky.

David crossed the street, out of the tilted shadow of the buildings into the bright park, walked to a large rock in the far corner and sat down on the grass beside it. One spot on the face of the rock just fit the curve of his back and he leaned back against the warmth the sun had left. Except perhaps for the front porch of his cabin, the rock in the corner of the park was David's favorite afternoon place to sit. From there he could watch the sunset stain the sky over the mountains and feel the lingering warmth. It was a good place to think.

Since his first childhood vacation in Henson, or rather, more likely because of it, David had been fascinated by the quiet authority of the mountains. He found himself drawn equally to their summits and their secret places, their crests and quiet spots, not so much conqueror as pilgrim, alternately exhilarated and intimidated by the awful exposure and soothed by a sort of privileged intimacy that he discovered there.

But it wasn't only the tempting topography of the mountains that stirred him. As much as their wildness and their bulk, what intrigued David about the mountains was the way they determined history, the effects they had on the lives of those men who attempted to come to terms with them, and it was that affection, that fascination, that had eventually brought David back to Henson.

It was his wife, Susan, who had convinced him to start writing the Hawthorne book. "Just do it," she had said impatiently one night after dinner. "You've talked about it for so long. Just do it!" It was just the sort of thing she would say. Cut to the chase. And on that day, he had begun. But that was before the accident.

Susan's death had completely overwhelmed David. It was a blow from a direction he had never expected and it nearly destroyed him. Angry and depressed, he quit his medical practice in New Hampshire and for a year isolated himself from his friends, wallowing in bitterness and melancholy, listless and alone, trying to find the end of the string, as he had put it. In the end, it was Susan that had saved him.

"Just do it. Just do it."

It was that two year-old echo that had awakened him that rainy afternoon. The next week he put his house on the market and moved to Henson.

The sun had been down behind the mountain for only half an hour and overhead the sky was still bright, but the close little valley was already in deep shadow. The strip of apricot stain just above the mountains was beginning to fade and the shreds of backlit clouds, so white all day, had turned gray. Across the street, the fuchsia neon of the Pine Cone Cafe sign blinked and buzzed. David could smell onions cooking, and hot oil and cumin.

He thought again about what Mary Hinsdale had said. Maybe the history of Henson was a good idea. There was plenty of material. The courthouse had a hundred and fifteen years of records on file and all the old back issues of the *Silver World* were still stored in the newspaper office. He was beginning to feel restless and uneasy. He had worked on the Hawthorne project in one way or another for nearly ten years, and he missed it. It had always been there for him to turn to, to read about, to add to. He had loved the chase. He would talk with Fuller about it when he got back from his sister's.

"Well," he said aloud as if talking to a companion, "there's always room for enchiladas." He got stiffly to his feet and started across the street toward the cafe. As he approached, he could hear the melancholy waltz time of a country juke box. He missed Susan. Still.

3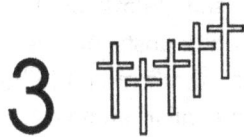

David and Fuller sat side by side on the wide cabin porch, their feet propped on the wooden railing, watching the day wear itself out. Beyond their boots, across the narrow gash of the valley, the pleated peaks of the main range of the San Juan Mountains rose abruptly into a series of pointed, stepped tiers spread out cross the horizon to the south.

David closed one eye, sighting over the toe of his boot and for a minute marked the slow, eastward progress of a bright cumulus cloud. When he could no longer keep the target centered, he inhaled deeply, breathing in the spicy fragrance of the sun-warmed spruce planking and, without lifting his head from the back of the chair, turned to face Fuller.

"I've got a better idea."

Without opening his eyes, Fuller shifted his weight slightly and recrossed his outstretched legs. "Better than what?"

"Better than a history of Henson County."

Ten seconds passed while David watched Fuller's face waiting for his response. Fuller stretched lazily, raised his head and squinted at David. "Well, do I have to guess ?"

David swung his feet down and leaned toward Fuller. "Alfred Hammit," he said, matter-of-factly.

"The cannibal?"

"Some said he was."

"And you?" Fuller asked with a sidelong glance.

"He denied it."

Fuller turned on his elbow to face his friend. "But he was convicted, wasn't he?"

"He was convicted of murder, but he denied that too."

Seeing that David was determined to discuss it, Fuller reluctantly sat forward in his chair and folded his hands. "What brought this up?" he said, trying to be patient.

"The grave site, I think," David replied. "I was by there again last night on the way home from the lake. I mean," he paused, palms up, thinking, "it's the matter-of-factness of it, isn't it? Just those six white posts and just enough chain to connect them. It's obviously a grave, and one that's meant to be noticed. But one headstone for five men? None with even similar names? And no explanation why they might have all died on the same day or what else besides a grave they might have had in common?"

"But everyone knows the story. At least everyone around here."

"You mean the legend," David suggested.

"Okay, the legend."

"It is a legend. That's just my point," David said, inching forward in his chair. "No one really knows what happened. It's true that Hammit was convicted of murdering those men but he denied it, even on his death bed. As for the cannibalism, he was never convicted of that, except by those who need legends."

"Don't we all?" Fuller said with the hint of a smile. "Okay," David nodded, "but you have to admit, it's a compelling story, isn't it?"

"No question."

"There are so many loose ends," David said, gesturing again. "Even as a kid I was fascinated by it. I think it was my favorite story. I never got tired of hearing it and my father loved telling it. Every year when we came here on vacation we went to the grave site, sometimes more than once, and while we were there he would always repeat the story. He was a great story teller." David smiled, remembering. "He would walk dramatically around the grave site, his voice rising and falling with tension, recreating their last desperate day, as he called it. It was as if the whole scene were playing out there before us. As if we were actually watching it happen. I could almost see the glow of their campfire in those trees by the river. Smell the smoke. And, like Hammit, I could—I remember my father's exact words—just make out, there in the failing light, those five sleeping forms curled against the cold. And when he described Hammit coming back to the campsite, I could actually hear Hammit parting the brush before him, hear his breathing and," David recited fondly, "hear the snow crunch under his hesitant step ."

"And," Fuller said, indulging him, "did he kill them?"

"Well," David answered with a shrug, "my father always used Hammit's version. The story Hammit told at the trial. That he came back from hunting, luckless and empty-handed again, to find Shannon Bell crouched by the fire, roasting the flesh he had cut from the five men he had killed in their sleep. When Hammit surprised him, Bell lunged at Hammit with a hatchet and Hammit killed him in self-defense."

"But, the jury didn't buy that?"

"No. Not at either trial."

"Either trial?"

"Hammit's attorney appealed the verdict of the first trial, based on some complicated jurisdictional point of law. I can't recall the details. But the appeal was granted and he was retried a year or two later."

Fuller sat for a moment, thinking, the fingers of one hand to his lips, his face turned slightly away. "Why," he said, turning directly back to David, "was Hammit in this valley in the middle of the winter?"

"Actually, they were headed for Breckenridge. Heard there was a big gold strike there. They were part of a larger party, twenty-five or so, that made up in Provo. They didn't leave Utah till November and it was January before they reached the Indian camp on the Uncompahgre River. Near Delta. Chief Ouray advised them to wait out the winter because of the unusually heavy snow in the mountains but they couldn't contain their impatience to finally get at their Golden Fleece. In early February Hammit and the five others left the Indian camp, according to Hammit, headed for a government cow camp about where Gunther is now."

"That's seventy-five miles," Fuller acknowledged.

"Right," said David. "Ouray said it would take them seven suns to reach it. From the cow camp they planned to go on another seventy-five miles to the Indian Agency at Los Pinos, and then out over Coalbank Pass to the Antonio Valley and from there up to Breckenridge. They were last seen headed in a southeasterly direction into a wind-driven snow storm."

"On foot?"

"They had one horse. At least, for one day they had a horse. A Tom Tracy went out with the other six for the first day. He helped pack them out with his horse but he turned back after about twenty miles when they reached the snow. That would have been somewhere between where Montrose and Cimarron are now. Hammit apparently intended to follow the Gunther River east to where the Los Alamos Creek entered it, then turn south up that river to the Indian Agency. It was snowing hard and Hammit said at his trial that the wind was sweeping the snow so deep in the gulches they had to follow the ridges. By keeping up on the ridges they may have become disoriented . . . that plus the poor visibility in the snow storm. When they came to the Lake Fork of the Gunther where it enters the main river I think Hammit thought it was the Los Alamos Creek and turned south one valley too soon. That led them into the Henson valley."

"Bad luck."

"In the wilderness there is no bad luck. Only bad judgment."

"Then you don't think Hammit led them up there to rob them," Fuller said.

"No. He was lost. I doubt Hammit, or anyone, would have risked his life for that. It was snowing constantly and they were freezing. They only had two blankets. They had run out of food. There was no game. I can't believe Hammit would have gone sixty miles out of the way in those conditions to rob them. If he had wanted that, he could have done it without coming all the way up into Henson valley."

"Mmmm," Fuller conceded.

"Next time you drive east along the Gunther River from Montrose, notice where the Lake Fork enters the main river. It looks almost identical to the place thirty miles farther on where the Los Alamos Creek enters. It would be easy to mistake the two, even in summer. I was out here one Christmas and hired a pilot from Gunther to fly me over the area so I could see what it looked like in the winter. Believe me, it's easy to see how they might have been confused in a blizzard. As a matter of fact, a group who set out from the Indian camp a few days after Hammit's group made the same mistake. They mistook the Lake Fork for the Alamos and went fifteen miles up the valley before they realized they had made the wrong turn."

"Why did Hammit keep going then?"

"I don't know, but he sure didn't seem to be enjoying the trip. According to his testimony, he seemed to think the Agency was nearby. The ridges they followed, trying to avoid the deep snow, took them higher and higher. When they turned south they were probably traveling along the high ground west of the Lake Fork, along the flank of Alpine Plateau. Even there the snow was so deep they had to take turns breaking a trail. They climbed to timberline where most of the snow had blown off. The traveling was easier but high up and ex-posed to the wind it was much colder. The only thing they could find to eat was rose hips and pine gum. By then they had been out sixteen days on a trip that was to have taken seven. They ate their moccasins. Burned the hair off and ate them. They craved salt. Hammit said they prayed and cried. At that point, they decided that they had to get down off of the mountain. Probably that was what's now called Red Cloud Peak. They went down to the spot where the bodies were eventually found."

"You pretty sure they came in from the north? Couldn't they have come in from the south, over Badger Pass or Alpine Pass?"

"Well," David nodded, "Hammit did say they came to a lake and, after crossing it, camped just below it. Crystal Lake is the only lake in the Henson valley and if they got to that first, they would have come in from the south. But the lake Hammit described was shallow. They tried to fish through the ice but there was only slime and mud. Doesn't sound like Crystal Lake. It's deep and over two miles long."

"Hmmm," Fuller agreed.

"They were probably camped where Acme Creek and the Lake Fork come together, at the upper end of the old Henson town site, near where the bodies were found. Settlers described beaver ponds in that area. Maybe Hammit's so-called lake was actually a beaver pond?"

"That means they may not have seen Crystal Lake at all."

" . . . and they didn't necessarily come in from the south," David finished.

"You have spent a lot of time on this, haven't you," Fuller said, somewhat surprised.

"I told you I liked trails," David said, smiling.

"And after the murders? How did Hammit go out after the murders?"

"He said he walked out to the west, over a mountain with a yellow mud slide. That has to be Slumgullion Slide. There's no place else like that in the valley and the slide area was just to the west of his campsite. It's a natural pass. From the summit he followed a stream, probably Los Alamos Creek, for thirty-five miles down to the Indian Agency. He said he tried every day to get over the pass but couldn't because the snow was too deep. Up to his armpits. It was April before sunny days and freezing nights made a crust he could travel on."

Fuller, arms folded, listened until David finished, then smiled, his hand to his mouth. It was a self-conscious gesture, a habit to hide teeth stained by the fluoride-rich water of his high plains ranch home. "Do you think Hammit murdered them?"

"Well," David said, "I'm not sure he killed them all. Maybe it did happen like Hammit said. But who knows? Maybe they were all in on it. Maybe they just killed off the weak ones, one at a time, and Hammit was the last?"

"Then he killed Bell?"

David nodded.

"And then he ate the bodies?"

David shrugged, smiling with mock innocence. "He was out for sixty-five days. He had to have eaten something. You can't live that long on moccasins and rose buds."

Fuller nodded knowingly then locked his fingers behind his head and looked out across the mountains. While they had been talking, the sun had moved over the peaks to the west and long shadows angled across the little valley below them and across Fuller's brown face, exaggerating the wrinkles around his eyes, as deep as scars. David watched Fuller as his companion sat thinking. He thought back how surprised he had been when they first met to see that Fuller, with his broad shoulders, flat butt and bandy legs, looked more like a cowboy than a college professor.

"Now that would be worth a story, wouldn't it?" David suggested.

Fuller lowered his hands and folded his arms across his chest. "You're right," he nodded, eyebrows arched slightly. "Actually, I'm surprised no one has done it before now."

"Am I convincing you?"

"You're beginning to."

"And we couldn't be in a better place for it. The transcript of the trial is still in the courthouse in Henson. I have seen it."

"It's still there?"

4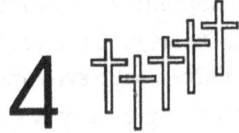

Bent at the waist, feet spread for balance, David sighted down the cue stick at the green nine ball snug against the far rail. With a slow, practiced rhythm, he slid the cue stick smoothly back and forth over the bridge of his left hand, plotting the angles in his mind. Angle of incidence equals angle of reflection. Physics is important after all, he thought to himself.

He paused, arm cocked, then stroked the cue ball smartly and watched it cross the table, striking the green ball to the left of center driving it into the bank. CLICK-THUMP. The struck ball caromed off the rail back across the table cleanly into the side pocket with a satisfying, leathery KA-LOCKA. The cue ball, its white energy spent, rolled slowly to the far end of the table and stopped six inches from the rail.

"Cross bank. Nice shot." David looked up to see Fuller standing beside him. Concentrating on the shot, David hadn't heard him approach.

"My favorite shot," David said, casually. "If you make it, everyone is impressed. If you miss it, well, it really wasn't expected, was it?"

"I'm impressed."

"How about a game to see who pays for dinner," David said, posing smugly, hands stacked before him on the standing cue stick.

"Not after that shot," Fuller conceded. He walked to one of the round tables in the center of the room, pulled out a chair and sat down. David put the cue stick in the rack on the wall and joined him.

The Pine Cone was Henson's only cafe. It had been a saloon during the the mining boom, a photograph behind the cash register was testimony to that. The same dark bar still ran along the west wall, half the length of the narrow room, and elk heads, perhaps the originals, still watched from the walls. The square tables in the photograph had been replaced with round ones, round ones with formica tops, and the pool table had been added and over it, the Olympia beer sign that hung suspended from the high, pressed-tin ceiling. But little else had changed about the Pine Cone since that August afternoon when

Larry Dothan had burst in breathless to announce that Alfred Hammit had been found guilty of murder and that the judge had sentenced him to hang.

"Hi, guys!" Dallas said, across the room. Dallas was the waitress and the bartender and the cook. She had large, happy, enthusiastic eyes and a smile that was an ad man's dream. At twenty-six she was doing exactly what she wanted to do and it was easy to tell that Henson was exactly where she wanted to be doing it. She rounded the end of the bar, a glass of ice water in each hand, and almost dancing, made her way through the empty tables toward them. Besides David and Fuller, the only other people in the cafe were two locals at the bar and one table of tourists who had strayed in looking for atmosphere and found instead, paper place mats and plastic glasses.

"And what does the chef recommend tonight?" Fuller asked.

Dallas laughed easily as she leaned between them with the water glasses." She says to try the tacos."

"Then that's what I'm having," said Fuller, looking to David.

"Me too," he said. "And a Dr. Pepper." David wanted a beer, but he never drank around Fuller. David wasn't sure alcohol had had anything to do with Fuller's leaving the college but from some of the things Fuller had said, it might have been. Anyway, he and Fuller didn't talk about it. Fuller would tell him when he was ready. They didn't talk about alcohol and they didn't talk about Susan. They had talked about a lot of things during the time they had known each other but not about feelings. It was a sort of operational understanding that had developed between the two men. No past pains, please. Off limits. Spare me the details.

"Iced tea for me," Fuller said.

Dallas turned toward the kitchen door. "Save some room for the peach cobbler," she called over her shoulder. "The cook says it's great."

"You may as well just bring it with the tacos," Fuller said. Without looking back, she waved acknowledgement.

Fuller turned to David and studied him, slightly bemused. "You know," he said, "I never actually knew anyone who drank Dr. Pepper."

David smiled. "It's always the coldest."

It wasn't the response Fuller had expected. "How do you figure that?"

"No one else likes it, so the cans stay in the cooler longer."

Dallas returned with another big smile and heavy white plates stacked up her arms. Without missing a beat, she skillfully set them down, two in front of David, two in front of Fuller, then stepped back, casually adjusted the rubber band holding her long hair, and propped her hands victoriously on her hips.

"OLE!" she said, with a quick flip of her chin.

"Ooo. Nice touch," Fuller said, applauding softly.

Dallas laughed with them, then suddenly secretive, leaned down between them, one hand on the back of each man's chair as if taking them into her confidence.

"*Gourmet Magazine* would kill for this taco recipe," she whispered, dramatically. She paused for effect, looking first at Fuller, then David.

My lips are sealed," Fuller whispered, playfully. David raised his hands, palms out, to confirm his innocence.

Then quickly changing character, Dallas straightened up, tilted her head slightly to one side, and smiling sweetly, fingertips together, oozed in a perfect, cloying parody, "En-joy."

The two men laughed again as she walked away.

"I know just the restaurant for you," Fuller called after her. "Bentwood furniture. And lots of ferns."

"Been there. Done that," she said, and flipping a towel over her shoulder, she disappeared into the kitchen.

David adjusted his plate slightly and then with a nod to Fuller, picked up a taco.

"You know," David said, gesturing with the taco, "She's got it. Frying the meat in the tortilla, that's the secret. Almost no one does that anymore. Now it's all identical, perfect, little mass-produced, preformed taco shells. Auto-Mex."

"Well, Taco Bell seems to be doing all right for itself," Fuller pointed out.

"Not for me," David said, chewing. "Give me the old-fashioned stuff. Like this. Brown. Hand-made. Disorderly. Lots of orange grease. And hot enough to make your forehead sweat. Right here." He tapped his forehead between his eyebrows.

Fuller touched his own forehead, testing.

"See what I mean? Fire and grease. Can't beat it."

They talked as they ate and when Dallas saw they had finished, she cleared the plates away, and brought coffee and refilled their cups twice without interrupting.

"It might be easier if we split up the work," David suggested. "I could go to the courthouse and review the transcript of the trial and you could check out the old newspaper accounts."

"I hope we have better luck this time," Fuller said. Two years before, David had gone to the Museum of New Mexico in Santa Fe in search of newspaper accounts of the Hawthorne Expedition only to find that all the issues from 1849 had mysteriously disappeared.

"I hadn't thought of that," David said. "I hope someone hasn't made off with these newspapers as well."

David was excited about working on another project with Fuller and he was eager to get started. He enjoyed the research but he particularly liked the writing. Sometimes it came easy for him. Like painting a fence, the words flowed smoothly onto the page and dried there. At other times, it was like building a stone wall, each word carefully sought out, then arranged and rearranged until its strength was perfect.

"Can you think of any other sources besides the trial transcript and the newspaper?" David asked.

"Relatives?"

"Maybe."

"A diary?"

"I'm not sure Hammit could write."

"What about the prison. They must have records of his personal effects."

"He didn't die in prison. Apparently he was released after serving only part of his sentence. He moved to Littleton where he died . . . a vegetarian, according to the legend," David added, hesitantly.

Fuller grimaced, slightly disgusted. "Surely that's a joke."

"Sorry," David shrugged, sheepishly.

"Well, maybe someone in Littleton could give us a lead?" Fuller made a mental note.

"I thought I might find you two here." The voice belonged to Dub Ponder. Dub was one of the one hundred and forty-four people living in Henson who had been born there. He and his wife Jolene had run the dude ranch above town for forty years. He limped slightly as he crossed the room toward them, favoring his right hip. The degree of his disability varied with the occasion.

"How'd you get loose from Jolene," David teased as Dub sat down. Jolene actually managed the ranch. Dub did the chores and kept the guests entertained telling stories.

"Golly Doc," Dub said, pushing the worn Stetson back with his thumb, "that woman's gonna' kill me. She's had me cleaning cabins all morning. It's a wonder this old body holds up." He winced as he shifted his weight in the chair

"I'll bet you've got strength enough left for fishing," David said.

"As a matter-of-fact," Dub said, his small eyes widening, "that's why I came looking for you two. We're going up to Heart Lake this evening and I thought you might want to go along. Lee and Buford just got back and said the fish were jumpin' in the boat."

"Will you have all the sheets done by then?" David said, laughing.

Dub took the joke kindly. "By golly Doc," he said as if he were actually confiding in him, "you know, I'm getting too old for this tourist business." He clasped his worn hands on the table in front of him. "Sometimes I wonder if it wouldn't be better just to shut 'er down and move to Moab."

"Why Moab?" Fuller asked.

"The kids are out there." Then he added with a resigned smile. "The ones that were gonna' stay and help us out around the place."

"You know you could never move to Moab," Fuller said.

"That's right, Dub," David added. "There's no fishing in Moab."

They didn't see Lomax come into the cafe. But they heard him. Lomax was laughing as he entered. It was a loud, disturbing laugh like street noises in the night. Lomax laughed a lot, too much, as if to alert anyone within earshot that as far as he was concerned everything he said was funny.

"Dallas, darlin', " Lomax called out as he strode over to the bar.

"I'm having withdrawal symptoms. How about bringing me the coldest bottle of Lone Star you can find?" Ed Lomax was a big man. He had the appearance of an aging professional athlete, overweight, but clearly muscular, with the easy, relaxed self-confidence of a celebrity, as if accustomed to being looked at, comfortable as the center of attention.

"We still don't have any Lone Star, Mr. Lomax," Dallas said, patiently. "You know, you're just going to have to start bringing your own. How about a Coors?"

"Colorado Koolaid!" he said disparagingly. "Make it a Coors then. When are you going to get some decent beer?" He laughed again and hitched the waist band of his belted slacks up and down with both hands, leaving it pretty much as it had been. It was a habit. A swagger. While Dallas was getting the beer, he turned to look around the room, not so much to see who was there, but to see who was watching him.

"Hey, Dub!" Lomax said loudly across the room. He winked theatrically at Dallas, picked up the beer bottle, and drinking from it as he walked, started toward the table where the three men sat. A heavy gold chain showed in the V of his open collared polo shirt. He walked up beside Dub's chair and put a plump hand heavily on his shoulder. The diamond-like stone in a large ring caught the light.

"You're looking good, Dub," Lomax said. "How's it going?"

"Good, Ed. Good," Dub replied with his usual enthusiasm, turning in his chair to look up at Lomax.

"Glad to hear it." Lomax said. "Glad to hear it."

"You know these fellows don't you? "Dub said gesturing to David and Fuller.

"I don't believe I have had the pleasure," Lomax said with forced sincerity.

"David Walton," Dub said, pointing to David. David half stood and reached over the table to shake Lomax's hand. "And Jack Fuller." Fuller nodded and made a barely perceptible acknowledgment with his hand.

"Pleased to meet you," Lomax said. "How'd you fellows get mixed up with this old bandit?" Lomax laughed, slapping Dub firmly on the back. David and Fuller smiled politely.

"How are things going up at the Golden Fleece?" Dub said to Lomax.

"Got lucky again, Dub," Lomax said. His attempt at modesty was unconvincing. "Sonny said the ore from number three tunnel is looking real good. Now if I can just keep that little sumbitch working."

The Golden Fleece had been one of Henson's richest mines during the boom days but it had closed down with the general collapse of mining at the turn of the century and had been idle until Lomax had bought the property the previous fall and hired a loner named Sonny Lott to work it for him.

"As a matter-of-fact," Lomax went on,"I just flew in to check on it. But right now," he said, glancing at the large watch on his wrist, "I've got to get up to the house." He leaned over the table and lowered his voice as if letting them in on a secret. "I'm meeting a couple of guys who might be interested in getting in on the action, if you know what I mean." He winked knowingly at Fuller. Fuller glanced sidelong at David.

"Well . . . ," Lomax said, finishing his beer and putting the bottle on the table. "I hate to leave good company but business calls. You know how it is." He put his hand on Dub's shoulder and gave it an uncomfortable squeeze. Dub winced. "Dub, ol' buddy, come by the house when you can?" The pitch of his voice rose at the end of the sentence, the inflection economically replacing the unspoken,"Okay?"

Lomax freed Dub and nodded to David and Fuller, "Gentlemen . . . ." He gave a sharp farewell salute, turned and walked toward the door. "Dallas, honey,"

5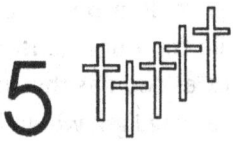

American Flats isn't flat. In truth, it's a glacial valley cut into the flank of Houghton Peak by the weight of twenty thousand centuries of packed blue ice. The valley slopes, but not steeply considering its location just at the timberline, eleven thousand feet above sea level. Everything is relative so to the prospectors who named it, men who spent their lives struggling against inclines and gravity, American Flats was the most nearly level ground around.

In this natural amphitheater, open to the north and shaded for all but the middle of the day, the protected snow pack melts slowly and the run-off keeps the valley floor moist all summer, conditions perfect for high-altitude wild flowers that thrive there, littering the ground like colorful confetti left from some summer celebration. Of all the mountains' secret rewards American Flats, with its technicolor surprise, was David's favorite.

American Flats is thirty miles from Henson, as the crow flies, on the opposite side of a geologic circle formed by two curved valleys. The circle, clearly visible on satellite photographs and topographical maps, marks the collar of a volcanic caldera, the collapsed remnant of a chain of volcanos that during thirty million years of periodic violence had covered the formative San Juans under a layer of ash and lava four miles thick.

Along the southern arc of this circle, a rough road climbs carefully through the fractured canyon, picking its way up along the headwaters of the Gunther River, turning like the river itself, past the ghost towns of Cleora and Ophir and Independence to Alpine Pass and the unmarked turn-off to American Flats. Beyond the summit of Alpine Pass the road circles back to the north, crosses the Divide again at Badger Pass, and descending onto the headwaters of Acme Creek follows the eager stream as it tumbles back toward Henson. It was a pilgrimage David made every summer.

David and Fuller left the cabin at seven o'clock. Fuller had driven down the night before so they could get an early start. They would need his jeep. Above the lake, the road to the high country narrowed to one track and without four-wheel drive it was impassable, even in dry weather. On the neglected mountain road, ten miles an hour was the best time they could expect and at that rate it would take three hours to make the thirty-mile trip from Henson to the Flats. David wanted to be in the valley by ten o'clock as soon as the sun cleared the peaks on the east side of the valley and the slanting light would be at the best angle for photography. The mornings there were almost always clear but often by afternoon, even in the summer, dark tattered clouds, like great, gray rags torn from the mountains by the wind, collected against the valley's curved cliff fencing, blocking the sun and blotting the vivid pigment from the painted ground.

On the plains and prairies, those wide level places of the world where horizons are stretched into thin tight lines, sunrise is dramatic and bold and the business of the day begins immediately with a bright orange hallelujah. A flatland dawn is an event, a point in time that can be noted on watches and digital clocks and recorded in the neat trustworthy tables of an almanac.

But morning comes more gently in the mountains. Here it is tactful and diffident and slow, and as David and Fuller drove away from the cabin toward the main road, this peaceful process had just begun. Overhead the sky was bright, already gone from gray to white to the blue of fresh enamel paint and the highest peaks, eager for the day, were tipped with light. But below these brilliant broken cones, lingering shadows, all that was left of the night, still filled the narrow valley like a soft light-gray fog. It would be almost another hour before the land, as if tipping along some unseen axis, tilted down below the level of the sun and the last of these dark stains drained away.

From the cabin road they turned south and at the junction just beyond Dub's ranch took the right-hand fork and bumped off the pavement onto the gravel surface of the lake road. They drove through the morning, soft and soundproof, past the dark and flawless lake. At its upper end, they turned up along the river that fed it and entered the canyon it had cut from the fluted cliffs. For two miles the road climbed slowly up out of the canyon and then, turning like the river itself, wound off across a broad alpine meadow toward the sloping crisscrossed flanks of the mountains that filled the perfect sky.

"I've never been back in here," Fuller said, shifting to a lower gear.

"I love this trip," David said. "I can never decide which side of the loop I like the best so I generally make a day of it, going up one side and coming back down the other. This road and the one up past your place come together over at Mineral Park on the other side of Alpine Pass." He unfolded a Forest Service map on his lap as he talked. "I should have brought you in here before."

32

"This road goes all the way to Silverdale?" Fuller asked.

"Right. It was one of Otto Meer's toll roads. He built it during the mining boom to connect Henson and Silverdale."

"That must be ninety miles."

"A hundred and forty miles, actually. All the way from the Antonio Valley to Silverdale. All hand labor. Well, mules and hand labor. It was finished in 1874, right after the Brunot Treaty was signed with the Utes. There wasn't much prospecting in here till the Indians were gone."

"I can understand that."

"Before Meers built this road the only other way into Silverdale from the Antonio Valley was up the headwaters of the Rio Grande over Cunningham Pass. Too rough for wagons. This road really opened up the area. People poured in. Lined the road day and night. Men with packs, on burros, and for the first time, in wagons. There," David said, pointing. "Down there. That's the old town site of Cleora."

Twisting up the valley towards Alpine Pass, the road had climbed up away from the stream that now looped five hundred feet below them. Fuller stopped on the shoulder of the rutted road and looked down on the narrow meadow. Along the center of the meadow was a string of five beaver ponds, burnished by the slanting light. Linked by the stream's watery braids, the five ponds—bright, flat, medallions—lay like a misplaced bracelet on the boggy ground. Near the lower pond at the foot of an angled talus slope, the cinnamon remnant of a lone log cabin, roofless and overgrown, tilted back against the incline that threatened it.

David folded one leg under him and sat on it to get a better view. "At the peak of the mining boom, a cloudburst took out the Black Wonder dam and the town with it. Before that, four hundred people lived there. Hard to believe now, isn't it? "

"It's nothing but a beaver bog," Fuller said.

"Perfect spot for beavers," David said. "Fifteen-degree incline."

"Fifteen degree incline?"

"Beavers always build their dams in streams with a fifteen degree drop. Any less and the water flow is too slow. Stagnant. Any steeper and the run-off washes the dams out."

Fuller looked at him skeptically.

"Honest," David said, turning his palms up. "Dub told me that. Ever see a beaver dam washed out?"

"Well . . . ."

"You never do. Beavers know." David smiled, and nodded authoritatively. "The ponds get silted up after a while, and the beavers move away, but you never see a beaver dam washed out."

Fuller thought about that for a moment, checked again to see if David was serious, then released the hand brake and drove away.

"When I was living in New Hampshire," David said as they drove, "some beavers built a dam in the little stream that ran right beside my office. When the fall rains came their pond threatened to flood the road so the game wardens came with a backhoe and knocked one end of the dam out. By the next morning the beavers had built it back again higher than before. At that point the wardens decided to trap the beavers and take out the dam. They planned to trap them live and take them off into the woods where they wouldn't cause any trouble. I went down to watch them set the trap. They opened what looked like a big, Samsonite suitcase and set it in the water just in front of the dam. The next morning, the trap was sprung closed, but was empty. The wardens reset the trap and the next morning found it sprung again and all that was inside was a stick of birch, gnawed on both ends. They set the trap a third time and when they came back the next morning the beavers had not only sprung the trap, they had incorporated it into the structure of the dam. Completely covered it with sticks and mud!"

"You're joking."

"I'm not," David assured him, his voice rising.

"I guess I would have never figured beavers had a sense of humor."

They drove on, climbing steadily through scattered stands of aspen and pine, past the weedy sites of Ophir and Sunnyside and Ashcroft, empty fields and parks, their streets gone to grass, their few brown buildings sway-backed and broken by the weight of a hundred winters, gat-toothed and scavenged for firewood or frames.

"The mines in here were small," David said over the engine noise. "The Highland Mary, Pride of the West, Polar Star, Ocean Wave, Yellow Medicine, Black Wonder, Legal Tender."

"Legal Tender. I like that ," Fuller said. "Great name."

"These claims in here were all staked on what they called float. Ore found on the surface. Hundreds of claims were filed before anyone realized how deep the veins ran. Then the legal battles started. There was a lot of fighting over boundary lines and overlapping claims. There was no way the Patent Office could keep up."

Beyond the meadows the valley narrowed to fifty yards and the road ran close along the stream. "This was the site of Independence," David said, indicating with his arm that he was referring to the strip of flat land between the canyon wall and the stream. "The big strike here was on July Fourth. 1875. The richest mines in the valley were in here. Independence was one of the telephone concert camps. A telephone line connected mining camps all through this area. On Sunday nights during the winter, all the camps listened in on the party line while the miners took turns entertaining each other singing, playing the accordion or the violin or a melodeon they carried from camp to camp on a burro."

The stone skeleton of an old rock foundation lay scattered down the slope on the north side of the valley. "That was the Smile of Fortune mill," David said. "How about that name?"

"These people were poets," Fuller said.

"All the old stamp mills were built down the face of a slope. The mine was up there," David said pointing up the side of the canyon. Fuller leaned across the jeep seat to look. "The ore came down to the mill in trams. Gravity took it down through the crushers. Concentration mills, they called them. The idea was to reduce the weight of the ore since it had to be hauled out to the smelter in wagons or on burros. Those foundations that look like steps supported tiers of huge rollers that crushed the rock as it moved down through the mill. At the bottom was a series of mesh wire screens where the dirt was washed away.

"Sounds pretty crude."

"Well, it reduced the weight but a lot of mineral was lost in the process. At best, only about half of the ore was recovered."

As he talked, David scanned the bare mountainside. Two thousand feet above the mill site near the timberline traces of abandoned foot-trails zig-zagged up across the talus slopes and feldfields to a score of ochre mine dumps just visible at the edge of the trees. For David those trails worn into the side of the mountain were a link with the past, as durable as an old melody, and he found himself slipping into an easy nostalgia, wondering again about the men who were compelled to compete for life at such a disadvantage.

When David came into the mountains, he didn't want to see people. He was much too possessive a lover to share. But he liked seeing the faded traces of man on the wild land. It was important for him that people had once been there, like benevolent ghosts warming the rooms of an old house. The majesty of the mountains required man's work for scale.

Just beyond the mill, a steep canyon opened to the north. At the head of the canyon, ten miles away, where the canyon's sloping sides met the horizon, the gray hook of Uncompahgre Peak poked up from the main range like a broken canine tooth. A single lenticular cloud, as if snagged in passing, rode motionless on the wind, suspended over the summit's nearly vertical eastern face.

Fuller leaned forward to start the jeep, then stopped and straightened up. "Where does that road go?" he asked, pointing. "That bridge looks new." Across the valley from the mill site a dirt track crossed the stream and disappeared up a wooded canyon.

"That's the road to the Golden Fleece," David said.

"Lomax's mine?" Fuller asked.

"Right. The main tunnel is five or six miles up that canyon."

"He trucks ore down out of there?"

"One dump truck load at at time, I guess. I've never been up there but I heard it's a bad road. Steep and dangerous. It's the original road. Dub said Lomax had it widened some with a bulldozer, but I guess there was only so much they could do. Dub told me when the mine was running the teamsters hauling the ore down chained the back wheels of the wagons and even dragged full-grown pine trees as brakes, but still wagons went off the road all the time. Mule teams and all."

"That canyon is probably filled with high grade ore," Fuller said.

"And bodies," David added. "The Million Dollar Grave Yard they call it."

Beyond Independence the road, now hardly more than a trail, climbed up through the sub-alpine growth zone, through the last stands of Englemann spruce and alpine fir and in the wet boggy shade bumped over the rotted corduroy of old logs. Just at the timberline the road crossed a long talus slope then wound over a series of grassy hummocks toward a sheer rock wall that rose for a thousand vertical feet and curved across the end of the valley a mile away. From the base of the wall, the road—at that distance a long, tan scratch mark—angled upward across the rock face at a forty-five degree angle toward the saddle between the peaks to the thirteen thousand foot summit of Alpine Pass.

Fuller steered slowly over the one-track shelf road, occasionally glancing quickly and uneasily down past the edge of the jeep and over the edge of the road into the valley below. From where he sat in the driver's seat it was nearly a straight drop of a hundred feet. At the base of the rock wall the road turned back on itself in a tight hairpin and started up the steep incline to the pass summit. A dirt track led off to the left and down over the bank.

"There," said David pointing. "Turn there."

Straining up in his seat to see over the hood, Fuller nosed the jeep care-fully down off the edge of the road and after traveling a hundred yards, David said, "Okay. Stop here." David turned to face Fuller. "Welcome to American Flats," he said, extending his arms from his sides, palms up.

Before them, the U-shaped valley sloped upward to a nearly perfect semi-circle of rock cliff that formed the walls of the cirque. Behind it and rising for another thousand feet was a row of stark, chiseled peaks, bare and gray except for long vertical fissures still whitened with last year's snow.

"Come on," David said getting out, "I want to show you something." Fuller followed over a rise and down to the edge of a small stream.

"How about that?" David said. There, along both sides of the stream the ground was covered with wildflowers—light and dark blue, white, yellow, fuchsia and purple—a multicolored mat thirty yards wide running back up the valley as far as they could see.

"I've never seen anything like this," Fuller said. "There must be fifty differ-ent kinds of flowers."

"I counted twenty-eight once. July is the best time to come. All the colors are out then. The yellow flowers bloom first, in late May. After that, purple. Then, in July, all the colors. Toward the end of the season, the order is reversed. The yellow are the last to go."

"There's no place you can put your feet without stepping on them," Fuller said as he made his way carefully down to the edge of the stream.

"I thought you'd be impressed I'll go get the stuff. Enjoy yourself."

Fuller walked along the stream stepping from rock to rock, stopping to look closely at the flowers. Absorbed, he didn't notice when David returned. David put the pack on the ground beside the stream, took out his camera and spent an hour taking pictures. The light was perfect, and in the wedge of sky above the valley, there was not a single cloud.

"Hungry yet?" David asked as he joined Fuller sitting on the stream bank. He rummaged through the pack and handed Fuller two sandwiches and a coke. "We should have put these in the stream," David said, gesturing with a coke can, "to keep them cold."

"How come you never brought me here before?" Fuller said.

"I wasn't sure you were ready," David joked.

"When I was still at the college," Fuller said, "I hiked into some places like this in the Elk Mountains but I never saw wildflowers this thick. I guess the closest thing to this would be in some of the valleys above Gothic."

"It must be a special microcosm here," David said. "Just the right amount of sunlight, just the right amount of water. At this altitude there is plenty of water and plenty of sunshine but it's unusual to have them both in the same place. I think Yankee Boy Basin near Telluride must be the same."

"Couldn't be any better than this," Fuller said.

"I don't see how," David agreed. "By the way," he said turning to Fuller, "you are sworn to secrecy, you know. Not many people know about this place."

"I'm surprised you didn't blindfold me," Fuller said sarcastically. "so I wouldn't know how we got here."

"I didn't think of it, actually," David said.

"I used to go fishing with an old fellow who did that."

"Blindfolded you!" David said, surprised.

"Worse than that. Before we turned off the main road he stopped the car and made me get in the trunk."

"Made you get in the trunk?" David asked, raising up on one elbow to see if he was serious.

"Yep," said Fuller matter-of-factly. "Going in and coming out."

David sat up. "You mean to tell me that you let someone talk you into getting in the trunk of a car, just to go fishing?"

"Every time," Fuller said.

"Every time!" David said, in disbelief. "You mean you went more than once?"

"What can I say," Fuller admitted with a shrug. "The fishing was good." Fuller laughed hard as David caught on to the joke and laughed with him.

The two friends sat in the sunny alpine valley for an hour. They talked and told stories, the gifts men friends give to each other and shared what they knew about the mountains. At 2:30, David glanced at the sky. A lenticular gray rain cloud had coalesced over the peaks at the head of the valley. That was important. The road down the other side of Alpine Pass crossed a series of high meadows which were often muddy and getting stuck, even in a jeep, was a greater danger than going over an embankment.

"We'd better get going," David said, nodding in the direction of the cloud. "There's something else I want to show you and we don't want to get rained on up here."

They packed up their gear, loaded the jeep and started back to the road.

"Go up here," David said, pointing to the shelf road that led up to the top of the pass."

"Over the pass? Have we got time?"

"I think so," David said, looking at the sky again. "If it gets too late I can stay at your place and you can drive me down in the morning." Fuller's cabin was on the Acme Creek road halfway between Badger Pass summit and Henson on the other side of the circular route they were taking. They would pass by it on the way back down to Henson.

The road to the top of the pass traversed the sheer rock wall face for a half a mile and just below its crest cut through a snowbank, higher than the jeep and dusted with wind-blown red dirt. Concentrating, Fuller sounded the jeep horn at the blind turns, a mountain-driving tradition, to alert anyone coming down the one-track road to look for a place wide enough for the two vehicles to pass.

At the top of the pass the jeep bounced roughly to a stop on a small rectangle of almost flat ground that marked the summit. A Forest Service sign indicated the altitude was 12,800 feet. They got out of the jeep and walked to the edge of the incline.

The summit was on the crest of a central pointed dome. Below them in all directions broken stained peaks and deep valleys fell away steeply in a radial drainage pattern to the tender pastels of the distance a hundred miles away. Except for a single cloud bank to the west, the view was unobstructed for 360 degrees.

"This is Oh! Point," David said. "This is what I wanted to show you."

Fuller turned slowly to take in the panorama.

"Henson is twenty miles or so down that valley," David said, pointing to the east. He swung his arm back to the northwest. "Ouray is there in the valley just beyond that ridge. When Hammit left the winter camp for the Indian Agency on Los Alamos Creek, he went along there." David traced a line along the horizon to the north. "Along the Gunther River valley just this side of Black Mesa. They turned from the main river at the Lake Fork and from there came into the Henson Valley. That had to be the route they took and the country fits the account Hammit gave at the trial. The only other way into Henson from Ouray is over this pass. Thirteen thousand feet? In a blizzard, with no snowshoes? Starving? I don't think it would have been possible."

"I see what you mean."

"It's hard to believe people lived and worked up here, isn't it?" David said. "I don't know how they did it, I mean working at this altitude."

"Maybe they were just born tougher than we are," Fuller said.

"I don't know," replied David. "Maybe it was a form of natural selection. I mean, by the time they had walked 1,500 miles across the country from the east coast, escaped every day from Indians and wild animals that were trying to kill them, survived living with thugs and thieves, dealt with the weather in all seasons and climbed up into places like this, probably the tough ones were the only ones left."

"Money is quite a motivator," Fuller said.

"If that's what motivated them. It may have been the money for some of them but I have a feeling others were just on the move. Drifters. Like Hammit."

"And Sonny Lott," Fuller added. "My guess is, he's on the move."

"You remember that story about Frenchy Carbazon recognizing Hammit in Wyoming three years after the massacre? Carbazon said he was sure it was Hammit when he saw that two of the fingers on his right hand were missing."

"I never heard that."

"Hammit worked at a mine in Georgetown for a while before he went to Utah. That was before pneumatic drills. The hard rock miners used hammers and hand drills to make holes for the charges. They worked in two-man teams. One man held the hand drill and the other hit it with a four pound hammer. Double jacking, it was called. In a dark, cramped mine tunnel . . . ."

"Don't tell me."

"You guessed it. Hammit got those fingers pounded off."

"Ouch!" said Fuller, flipping his hand in feigned pain.

A quick, cool wind swirled the dust around their feet. They looked at the sky and hurried to the jeep just as the first large drops of cold rain began spattering on the windshield. The gray cloud bank had darkened and, drifting slowly east, had met them at the summit.

6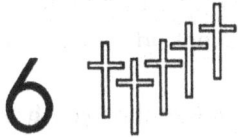

Shifting into low, Fuller steered carefully down the backside of the pass. The rain picked up quickly and driven by the wind, drummed on the canvas top and pounded onto the windshield and leaked around the side curtains onto the floor. Straining forward to see Fuller eased the jeep over the wet road, picking his way carefully around rocks and deep holes. The windshield wipers whined and thumped a rhythmic tattoo.

The slope on the back side of the pass was much less than the ascent from the east but the road was already muddy and getting worse fast. Aspen poles marked the edges of the road at regular intervals. Without them in a summer snow storm it would be impossible to find the track across the treeless alpine terrain and off the roadbed on the boggy ground, a vehicle, even a jeep, would be stuck up to the axles in no time.

From the summit of Alpine Pass it took an hour to reach the abandoned site of Mineral Center. Without stopping they turned east and started up. The rain continued and water stood in puddles on the yellow clay.

"I don't like this side of Badger Pass," said David. "This clay is so slick." David had been over the pass many times and was well aware of the dangers, especially when the road was wet. Descending the steep pass with too much momentum it was easy to slide on the slippery clay and more than one jeep had gone over the edge at one of the hairpin turns.

Coming up, especially in the rain, getting stuck was the risk. That often meant either making a fast run at the mud hole, trying at the same time to keep the jeep from bouncing out of control, or backing down the narrow wet incline for a quarter mile or more to a place wide enough to turn around.

On the exposed mountainside high above the tree line the wind, noisy and threatening, shook the side curtains and swirled thick clouds around them, limiting viability to a few yards. David knew that, at that altitude, the rain might turn to snow, making the traction even worse.

"Keep up your momentum," he said, trying to mask his concern.

The jeep, rocking and pitching, groaned up and around a steep switch-back. "I sure hope we don't meet anybody," Fuller said, straining to see. "There's no room here to pass anywhere."

"If we do meet someone" said David, "remember, you have the right of way. The climbing car always has the right of way."

"I'll keep that in mind," Fuller said weakly.

Slowly they wound up the steep pass, moving only slightly faster than a walk. At times the hairpin turns were so sharp, that Fuller had to stop the jeep halfway through the turn and back up a few yards to make a straighter pass at the turn, all four wheels spinning in the mud as the jeep strained to start up the steep incline. There were no other vehicles. Both men were relieved.

They crossed the barren summit without stopping, and by the time they reached the timberline, the rain had stopped. In an hour the road would be blowing dust again.

"Look at that," David said, leaning to see back up the mountain. New snow covered the the peaks behind them. "We got down from there just in time."

"It got hostile up there in a hurry."

"And this is July," said David. "Just imagine poor ol' Hammit trying to come through this country in the winter."

"I can't imagine it."

By the time they got to Fuller's cabin it was nearly six o'clock and even though it was July, the mountain air was cooling quickly. Fuller built a fire and the two men sat talking, watching through the window as the valley darkened. It was nine o'clock before they ate and midnight before they went to bed.

"Did you know Hammit had epilepsy?" David said into the darkness.

"No, where did you hear that?"

"It came out at his trial. I remember it from the transcript. On the trip from Utah a man named McGrue shared a bedroll with Hammit. Apparently no one else would. He said Hammit often had seizures in the night and he, McGrue, would hold him like a sick child until the seizure stopped."

"Hammit probably never knew that."

"I doubt it. McGrue didn't say. But he did say he thought that was one reason the other men hated Hammit."

"Hated him?"

"That was McGrue's word."
"Hated him because he was different."
"Exactly"
"That must have influenced their testimony at the trial."
"Almost certainly."

7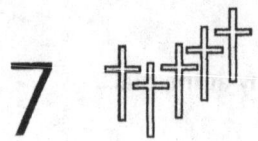

David, still in fishing waders, sat on the smooth rocks of the stream bank leaning against an old pine root, his feet in the clear water. It was getting dark and he knew Fuller would be along any minute. They had been fishing a quarter of a mile apart all afternoon, making their way slowly upstream. David was the first to reach the spot where they left the car.

Narrowed and accelerated by the close canyon walls, the stream at his feet poured noisily through the rocks for thirty yards before it broadened out into a deep pool, then curved to the left around a point of rocks and out of sight. David had caught two large brown trout in the pool on his way upstream, and he was still watching the slick surface for rises when he spotted Fuller come around the corner. He was carrying his rod by the handle, tip pointing backward to avoid sticking it into the rocks if he stumbled. David watched as he walked toward him, making his way carefully along the rocky stream bank.

"Well, old fellow," David said as he approached. "Ready to call it a day?" Fuller sat down heavily beside David.

"Just about," Fuller puffed. "How did you do?"

"It was pretty slow until after 3:30, but it picked up after that. How about you?"

"Same thing," Fuller said "Just about 3:30. As soon as there was some shadow on the water. After that any fly with yellow on it worked." Neither one mentioned the number or the size of the fish they caught. They had fished together enough that they no longer felt compelled to compete.

"Did you see anyone else fishing?" David asked.

"Only one fellow at the bridge."

"How was he doing?"

"I didn't ask," said Fuller. "He was using wet flies"

"Hmmm" said David. They had agreed they were both bigots as far as dry-fly fishing was concerned. They preferred the demanding casting that dry-fly fishing required. They preferred watching the fly on the water, preferred seeing the fish strike, rather than feeling it happen somewhere under the water.

"Well," said David getting stiffly to his feet, "If you're finished, I'd say the only thing that would make this day better would be a few fajitas."

"My friend," Fuller said, standing up beside him, "I'd say you've read my mind again."

They walked up the bank and through the willows and alder bushes to the car. The narrow river canyon was completely shaded and the damp earthy musk of the alders was strong in the cool air of the evening. David opened the trunk and they sat on the bumper replaying the afternoon as they removed waders, broke down rods and put their gear away. Neither had kept any fish. They seldom did. Neither even used a creel. They routinely used flies from which they had filed the hook barbs so the fish could be released without injury.

David started the engine and drove slowly through the alders along the overgrown dirt track that led to the main road. As they approached the shoulder, a brown pickup rounded the corner and passed in front of them headed north.

"Wasn't that Sonny Lott's?" David said, stopping the car.

"Probably headed up to Gunther to see his girlfriend."

"Or . . .?" David said, mischievously."

"Or what?" Fuller asked

"Don't you remember what Dub said about thinking that Sonny was running dope? Maybe he's on a buy, or a delivery?"

Fuller frowned skeptically.

"Come on, let's follow him," David suggested with a newly found energy.

"But, Gunther's an hour's drive," Fuller complained, "and I'm starving."

David reached into his pocket, retrieved two candy bars and held them up to Fuller. "Snickers, Sherlock?" David offered with a grin.

Fuller, at first reluctant, then resigned, took one of the candy bars. "It's a deal, Watson."

David turned up onto the road. Sonny's pickup was out of sight. Twilight was rapidly becoming darkness.

"You think he saw us?" David said as he accelerated along the river road.

"I doubt it," Fuller replied. "If he did, there's nothing suspicious about a couple of fishermen. Just keep well back of him. There's probably no one else on this road this time of night. We can catch up to him later, closer to town."

For the first thirty miles the road followed the winding river canyon, and during that part of the drive David and Fuller never saw the pickup, but there were no turn-offs and they were sure Sonny was still up ahead. At the Portal a gate-like rock formation marked the end of the canyon. Here the road left the river, bearing to the east side of the valley where it passed over a series of low sage hills. The sky and land were black. There was no horizon. In the distance David and Fuller could see taillights, two red dots, small and close together.

"There he is," they said at the same time. They drove on through the darkness, following the little pair of lights that slowly rose and fell in and out of sight over the invisible contours of the land like the running lights of a ship riding the swells of a heavy sea.

"How much farther to the intersection," Fuller asked.

David glanced at the speedometer. "About another ten miles," David answered. "The road straightens out about a mile before the intersection so we should be able to get a better idea how far we are behind him. After he turns I'll get closer so we won't lose him going through town."

"Right," said Fuller.

They rode in silence for another ten minutes. Cresting a low rise, the road descended toward the intersection a mile away. The pickup's taillights brightened as it braked to a stop. Then after a brief pause the brightness diminished, but instead of turning right toward Gunther, the lights swung to the left and accelerated up a long hill and out of sight."

"Ho-o-o-o," David said, surprised. He pulled the car over onto the shoulder of the road and stopped. He turned to Fuller.

"What do you make of that?"

"So much for the story of the girlfriend in Gunther," said Fuller.

"Maybe the girlfriend lives in Montrose," David suggested.

"Or maybe we just picked the wrong night to follow him?" The two men sat thinking.

"Well, what do you want to do now?" said David.

"Well," said Fuller, "unless I miss my guess, right now you are thinking about going on into Gunther to the A&W drive-in for a cheeseburger and a root beer float."

"What would make you think a thing like that?" said David.

"Just a lucky guess."

*　　　*　　　*

It was 10:45 before they started back to Henson. Both men were tired and just after leaving Gunther Fuller leaned his head back against the seat and slept. He didn't wake up until the car rumbled across the cattle guard just north of Henson.

"Well," Fuller said stretching, "so much for the detective work. Maybe we should confine our sleuthing to the library?"

"It would be interesting to know where he was going, wouldn't it?" said David as they drove through the dark town. The streets were deserted. Even the Pine Cone lights were out.

"You've been reading too many mystery books," Fuller said.

"Maybe so," said David, "but if Sonny was really going to see his girlfriend, why bother to go to all the trouble to come back so early in the morning. Why go and come in the dark? It's almost as if he was deliberately trying to avoid attracting attention."

"Well," said Fuller, "if that's the case he sure doesn't know much about small towns. The surest way to attract attention in a small town is to do something a little different. And do it over and over again."

"You have to admit," David said, refusing to give up on it, "it is a little curious that his trips are so regular, and that he stays gone for the same time each trip. It suggests he is going to the same place, and that place doesn't seem to be Gunther."

"Maybe this wasn't one of his typical trips," Fuller said.

"Maybe so," replied David.

Two miles beyond town David turned left onto a side road, crossed the wooden bridge over the river and drove up the hill to his cabin. He stopped by the back door and switched off the engine.

"It's late. You want to stay here tonight?" David said turning to Fuller.

"Oh, thanks," Fuller said, "but I'd better get going. I promised Dallas I would come over in the morning and fix that gate for her."

"Well, give me a call when you're finished," David said.

"I'd like to go back down to the river. I lost a couple of nice fish in that pool just below the falls."

"Enough's never enough, is it?" Fuller grinned.

"Call me."

David watched Fuller drive away, then went inside and dressed for bed. For a few minutes, he sat on the edge of the bed, thinking. Just before he turned out the light, he took the clock from the bedside table and set the alarm for five o'clock.

8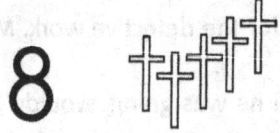

It was still dark when the alarm went off. David silenced the buzzer and sat up on the edge of the bed. It was a hour till daylight. That was plenty of time to get to the park.

He switched on the light, walked into the kitchen and lit the stove. He put on the coffee pot and while it perked took a quick shower. Then he dressed, filled a thermos with coffee and went out to the car. The darkness was still and cool, stars hard and bright as barn lights.

He drove the two miles to town and parked the car out of sight in the alley behind the Pine Cone. There were no other cars on the streets and at that hour the only sign of life was the single bare bulb in front of the post office at the far end of the main road. David crossed the street and sat on the grass beside the large rock in the corner of the park. From there he could see anyone driving up the main street from Gunther. He poured a cup of coffee from the thermos, leaned back against the rock and waited.

The sky was just getting white over the mountains when David heard the sound, a low and distant hum at first, then louder as it approached. Two minutes later Sonny's pickup passed slowly by the corner of the park and continued out of town to the south. David looked at his watch. It was 6:05. Sonny Lott had been gone—somewhere—for nine hours.

When the sound of the motor had died away, David got in his car and drove home, anxious to tell Fuller what he had learned. He would wait for Fuller to call.

At the cabin David took out a map of the western United States and un-folded it on the kitchen table. He tied a piece of string to a pencil and lay the string along the map key. He measured off 250 miles and tied a small knot in the string at that point. With one finger he held the knot down on Henson, stretched the string tight and with the pencil drew an arc on the map, north to south. The line curved downward from Wyoming across the center of Utah and Arizona to New Mexico and marked the approximate range—round

48

trip—of someone driving for nine hours at fifty-five miles an hour. He sat back, arms folded across his chest, and studied the map.

The night they had followed Sonny he had turned west at the intersection, toward Montrose and Grand Junction. At Grand Junction, there would have been three choices. If he had continued west, Highway 50 led to Provo and Salt Lake. Turning north, he could have reached Green River, Wyoming. To the south, he might have gone as far as Gallup or Tuba City or Lake Powell. Then, of course, he could have stopped anywhere along the way in an area of 80,000 square miles, a landmass the size of New England and upstate New York combined. Not much help, David thought. Maybe Fuller will have an idea.

At ten o'clock the phone rang.

"He was gone for nine hours," David said, matter-of-factly.

"What?" said Fuller. It was not what he had expected to hear.

"Sonny drove back into Henson at 6:05 this morning. That means he was gone for nine hours."

"You actually watched him?" Fuller said with surprise.

"I was sitting in the park when he drove by."

"Are you sure it was Sonny?" Fuller asked.

"I'm sure of it," David said flatly. "Brown pickup. Dual rear wheels."

"You're really taking this seriously, aren't you? Where do you think he went?"

"I don't know. Come on over and I'll show you the possibilities on the map."

While David waited, he took a walk along the river. There was a heavy hatch of Mayflies, hovering in their characteristic columnar formations, and a few trout were rising. He sat for a while in the cool sunshine and listened to the river's smooth music. David knew this stretch of river well. It was here, forty years ago, after he was tall enough that his father had taught him to fly cast with a nine-foot bamboo rod and a church hymnal under his casting arm to keep his elbow at his side.

"Let the rod do the work, son."

David could see his father there beside him, overfilling his matching khaki shirt and pants, the Frank Buck pith helmet shading his indoor face as he counted out the slow cadence of the cast that would eventually become instinctive, and that he still, occasionally, found himself silently mouthing.

"Bangor is a nice city. Bangor is a nice city."

It was on this same stretch that he learned to read the water, learned about riffles and pool-tails and current-shear and what they can do to a floating flyline. It was here he had learned where fish live and how to present a dry fly across the laminar flow of the current so it would drift lifelike, irresistible, just over their unseen noses. Here he had learned to double-haul, how to cast in the wind, how to shoot the line from hand held coils and how to stop it short with a pinch of his index finger to drop the fly onto the water as softly and naturally as a piece of cottonwood down and it was here he had learned to fish pocketwater and how to mend the line cast across the current to get a five second, drag free drift on the surface of a deep, slick pool.

Funny, he thought. Five seconds is such a natural common denominator for things that men put into motion. Five seconds is the hang time of an NFL punt, of a well hit tee shot and the time you have to put on a drag free drift if you want to fool an old hook-jawed brown trout.

But for David the quiet private pleasure of dry fly fishing had very little to do with trophy fish or technique or bag limits or filled creels. It had more to do with—if it could be reduced to just two things—the sound that moving water made and the fact that flyfishing was one of the few things you could stay at all day and in the end realize that you hadn't stopped for lunch.

Just before noon he returned to the cabin and heated chili and tamales, opening the cans and putting them directly on the stove burner. Fuller was always amused by this bachelor practice, but David said it made cleaning up easier. He was sitting on the porch watching a squadron of swallows practice their aerobatics when Fuller drove up.

"Hungry?" David asked, as Fuller got out of the jeep.

"It's lunchtime, isn't it?" Fuller replied flatly.

"Come on in and I'll show you the map while we eat."

He followed David into the house and sat at the table. David spooned chili and tamales onto two plates and set them down on the map, one plate on Texas and the other on California.

"No beans?" Fuller said with a smile as he explored the chili with his spoon.

"You know better than to ask that," David answered. David insisted that real chili didn't have beans in it. It was all right to have beans on the same plate, but never actually in the chili.

"Well," said Fuller looking at the map. "Let's see what you have done."

David leaned over the map. "Well," he began, "the way I figure it took Sonny one hour to go from Henson to the intersection. And one hour on the way back. That leaves seven hours. If he drove fifty-five miles an hour for three and a half more hours he could have gone as far as this." David pointed with his spoon to his arc on the map. Fuller leaned closer.

"Not much out here. Just white space"

"I know," said David. "That's what bothers me."

Fuller tapped his lips gently with his spoon, thinking. "What about Salt Lake City?"

"He could have gone that far if he was headed for a big town."

"Mmmm," Fuller muttered. "Otherwise, anywhere in here." He moved his hand over the large penciled area.

"Not much help, is it?" David said.

"Not a lot," Fuller agreed. The two sat eating, studying the map.

"There is one thing."

"What's that?"

"There are lots of places to land an airplane out here," David said, tapping the white space on the map."Suppose he met a plane? Someone flying drugs up from Mexico?"

"Fine," said Fuller. "But then what?"

"Maybe he met the plane and then delivered the drugs to, say . . . Salt Lake City?"

"Too many possibilities, aren't there?" Fuller said. "Besides," he added somewhat impatiently, "we're getting all worked up over nothing. There's nothing but Dub's hunch that Sonny is dealing drugs. Sonny probably just went to Montrose."

"Well," Fuller said, "there is one way to settle it, isn't there?"

"Follow him? I thought you were bored with that?"

"It's the only way to know, isn't it?"

*   *   *

On Wednesday evening, David and Fuller drove to Gunther. It was eight o'clock by the time they got to at the intersection west of town. David turned west toward Montrose, drove to the top of the hill and pulled into a roadside park. He stopped the car thirty yards away facing the road. Back to the south and below them they could see the intersection, and beyond that the last mile of the road from Henson.

While waiting, they talked and watched the sun set behind the silhouette of the Uncompahgre Plateau forty miles away. David felt uneasy. Perhaps he had been too impulsive. He thought Fuller seemed uneasy too.

Just before dark a pair of headlights came over the hill from Henson and sloped down to the intersection. David watched through binoculars as the lights stopped, then turned east toward Gunther.

"Jeep," David noted.

Half an hour passed. At 9:30 headlights appeared again at the top of the hill.

"Right on schedule," David said, raising the binoculars and focusing on the lighted area where the two roads came together. "It's a pickup," David said, as the truck slowed to a stop in the bright circle. "Dual rear wheels."

Fuller leaned forward straining to see. "Brown?"

"Can't tell," David said, "but it's headed this way."

The truck turned toward them swinging its lights in an arc through the darkness and started up the hill in their direction. At the top of the hill, the road angled slightly away from the roadside park. David's car would be hidden in the darkness.

"Is it Sonny?" Fuller asked, as the truck sped past them.

"There's just one person."

"A man?"

"I can't be sure," said David putting down the binoculars, "but I'll bet it's him. Let's go see." David leaned forward to the ignition.

Fuller stopped him. "You sure you want to do this?"

The key still in place, David turned to him. "I think so."

David started the car, waited till the pickup lights were out of sight then switched on the headlights and pulled onto the highway.

"You know," said Fuller, as David accelerated, "if you had told me a week ago I would be chasing a drug dealer through the night across southern Colorado I would have called you a liar."

"Me too," said David, nodding slowly.

For the first ten miles they followed the truck's lights through the river valley along the southern flank of Black Mesa. There was no traffic on the dark road and it was easy to keep the truck in sight. David kept pace, following close enough to see if the truck turned off the road, but far enough back to avoid suspicion.

At Sapinero the river entered the canyon and the road crossed up onto the foothills of the Alpine Plateau where the turnings hid the truck from view for several minutes at a time. David sped up and closed the gap. For ten minutes, neither man spoke.

"There's Montrose," Fuller said. Five miles away the lights of Montrose cast a pale yellow glow in the night sky.

"And there's Sonny," Fuller said. A mile ahead of them the truck's lights came into view, still headed west. Nearer town David pulled up to within a hundred yards of the truck. Lights from the peripheral buildings of the little town—service stations, convenience stores, body shops—spilled across the highway and illuminated the brown truck as it passed, silhouetting the driver against the lighted pavement.

"It's Sonny all right," said Fuller, a trace of excitement in his voice. "Baseball cap and pony tail."

The pickup slowed at a blinking yellow light, then turned right along the main street. David slowed and dropped back behind a jeep to separate his car from Sonny's truck.

"Do you think he's suspicious?" asked David.

"He doesn't act like it," replied Fuller."If he turns, go on to the next block and turn back." David was surprised at Fuller's growing enthusiasm.

But Sonny never turned. He never even slowed down. He drove straight on through the business district and on past the edge of town accelerating into the night beyond the lights.

"We must have spooked him," Fuller said.

"Either that or he's headed to Grand Junction. What time is it?"

"Ten o'clock."

"Well," said David, "looks like we're going to Grand Junction."

"That's thirty miles."

David turned to his friend. "What else have you got to do?"

The highway was good and the thirty mile drive took only half an hour. As they approached Grand Junction, they could see the lights of cars on interstate 70 crossing over the road in front of them. The pickup moved to the right lane, by-passed the turn-off to Grand Junction and headed up the ramp to merge with traffic headed west.

"That's enough for me!" David said, turning off toward Grand Junction.

"I'll be damned," said Fuller, provoked. "Where is he going?"

David pulled the car over and stopped. He switched on the interior light. "Well," he said, unfolding a map, "at least we know he's heading west."

"And, that he didn't go to Montrose," Fuller added.

David studied the map on the seat between them. "One hour to Gunther, another to here—that leaves seven hours to get to where he's going and back to Henson by six. That means the turnaround point is no more than a three and a half hour drive from here. Traveling fast, he could get to Provo."

"Or anywhere down here." Fuller was pointing to a large white space on the map. There, south of Green River, were the canyonlands of Utah, ten thousand square miles of buttes and mesas and slick rock canyons as sparsely populated as any place on earth.

"Well," said Fuller, "it wouldn't do any good to try to follow him there anyway. On that flat land he could see us coming for ten miles."

David reluctantly agreed.

"Runners One. Chasers Zip." said Fuller.

"What now?"

"Well," Fuller replied, holding his watch to the light, "it's 10:30. It's two hours back to Henson. It's been a long day. Suppose we call it quits and find a nice motel?"

"I guess you're right," David said. "I just hate giving up on it after coming this far." He gripped the steering wheel with both hands and stretched. "Won't Dub be pleased?" David said, nodding to himself. He turned to see Fuller smiling.

"You can't wait to tell him, can you?"

9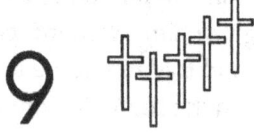

Sonny Lott was a loser. Losing was a way of life that had embittered him and it taunted him every day like a painful limp. The loser image had shaped his life and it took form in the crude five-lettered tattoo on the back of his left hand. He had done the job himself with a fountain pen because he didn't have the fifteen dollars to pay someone else to do it. Twenty-five years old and too poor to have LOSER tattooed on his hand.

Sonny had never been able to adjust to the expectations of life. At thirteen, when he quit school, no one cared. Two years later he ran away from home and hitch-hiked across the country, drifting from state to state, working carnivals and construction. He learned the hard way that at five foot eight inches and one hundred forty pounds, he was too small to strike out physically at the world he felt had cheated him. His rage took the form of theft, a secret faceless revenge.

In the ten years since he had left home, Sonny had made some bad mistakes, but perhaps the worst mistake of all had been breaking into Ed Lomax's house. If he had thought about it, he would have realized Lomax had seen him too often in the neighborhood when he was checking out the house.

He had been surprised, that night, when he found the door of Lomax's house unlocked and he had been more surprised that there was no security alarm. But his biggest surprise had come when he entered Lomax's dark bedroom and the light had snapped on unexpectedly. There was Lomax sitting in the middle of the bed, a chrome plated pistol in his outstretched hands, leveled at Sonny's face. It was as if Lomax had trapped him.

Lomax had handcuffed him and Sonny thought they were going to the police station. Instead, Lomax had taken him to the garage where he chained his hand to a metal post. Lomax had photographed him with a Polaroid camera, taking two extra shots, and with a sardonic grin had tucked one into Sonny's shirt pocket. For a week he had been handcuffed in the garage, Lomax feeding him hamburgers and Koolaid. Then he was offered the deal.

"Work for me at the mine," Lomax had said, "or go to jail."

It had been an easy choice. Another breaking and entering charge would have put him away for forty years. Lomax had given him two hundred dollars in cash, a map and the keys to the brown pickup and told him to be in Henson in four days or he would tell the police he had stolen the truck. So Sonny Lott went to Henson and that is how he found himself alone, in the damp, narrow darkness of the Golden Fleece mine's tunnel Number Three.

Sonny gently tamped the last charge into the hole, adjusted the head lamp beam, and stepped back to inspect his work. When he was satisfied, he set the radio frequency trigger and headed for the tunnel entrance six hundred feet away.

It took him four minutes, stooping under the low places and stepping over puddles of rusty water that had collected on the tunnel floor. Sonny had learned about blasting from working on construction. He knew that the way he had placed the charges, the blast would shear off half a ton of rock, breaking it into pieces small enough to be mucked into the ore car that ran on tracks out to the mine dump. In a split second he would generate two days' work. Squinting in the bright sunlight, he walked from the tunnel to the cabin, sat on the porch and lit a cigarette.

The mine site, wedged into the apex of a narrow canyon, looked pretty much as it did when the last of the company miners had walked off the job seventy-five years before. The tunnel had been cut into the base of a sheer rock outcropping and from out of this slanted black rectangle, a pair of rusty iron rails tracked a hundred feet across the pile of broken yellow rock to the dump truck which had been backed into position below the end of the rails. To the right of the tunnel entrance the little box of a cabin, weathered the color of the rusty rails and slightly off plumb, leaned against the slope of the canyon wall. The cabin door and the two small windows had been replaced and the low roof patched in one place near the chimney with four unmatched green asphalt shingles. Otherwise, only the trash pile was new.

From the porch Sonny could look back down the canyon into the river valley two thousand feet below, and beyond that to the angular geometry of the peaks stacked across the horizon to the north. He flicked away his cigarette and checked the frequency of the radio transmitter. Blasting had always given him a sense of satisfaction, being able to do so much damage at a distance and with so little effort. It made him feel powerful, like the big men he envied and resented. Blasting was like carrying a gun. It was an equalizer.

He flipped on the switch and activated the detonator. At that instant, he felt the ground-shock from inside the tunnel, followed immediately by a muffled blast. For an hour he sat on the cabin porch waiting for the dust to settle in the tunnel. Then, switching on his head lamp, he walked back into the mine, pushing the ore car along the track in front of him.

The rest of the afternoon he shoveled the broken rock into the ore car, pushing it out to the end of the dump and emptying it into the dump truck below. As he brought out each load, he stopped at the tunnel entrance and sorted through the rock, picking out five or six of the heavier darker chunks that he knew were almost pure mineral. He added these to the pile near the entrance. Later he would take these to the cabin and put them under the floorboards with the others.

By Friday the dump truck would be full and he could drive to the smelter in Salt Lake City where the ore would be weighed, graded and sold and the proceeds mailed to Argonaut Enterprises. But before that, he had another trip to make.

The next day, Sonny loaded the ore from under the floor boards into the back of the pickup. It would hold about a ton of ore and so far that had yielded about five hundred dollars a trip. He ate supper, then snapped the tono cover down over the truck bed, concealing the rock cargo. Just before dark he locked the cabin and started down the steep road to town.

By the time he reached Henson the stores were closed and the suppertime streets were empty. He drove through town to the post office. There was still no check from Lomax. He drove around the park. There were several cars at the Pine Cone, but no one on the street and as far as he could tell, no particular attention had been paid to the heavily loaded brown pickup.

On some of these night time trips, before he returned to Henson, he snapped the tono cover in place over the empty truck bed. Occasionally he brought back a load of firewood and sometimes, just to mix it up in case he was being watched, he returned with the empty truck bed open.

When he reached the cattle guard at the north end of town he pulled over to the side of the road, got out and went through the motions of checking the tires. Looking over the hood of the truck he could see Lomax's house on the hill across the river. There were no lights. Satisfied, he got back in and started down the canyon toward Gunther and the highway intersection.

In the failing light, he didn't notice the two fishermen sitting in the car parked in the alders by the river.

10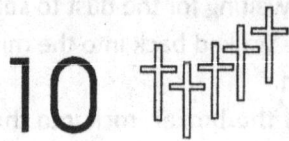

"Have some more cobbler." Dub's wife motioned to the Pyrex bowl in the center of the table.

"Oh, no thanks," David said, leaning back in his chair. "I'm fine."

"I'll put the rest up for you to take home." She smiled and reached for the dish.

"Hey!" Dub protested with mock indignation. "What about me?"

"I'd say you get pretty well taken care of," she replied to Dub, scolding him gently. The two men laughed.

"It was a great dinner," David said to Mrs. Ponder. "Thanks very much."

She smiled appreciatively. "Well, you need a home-cooked dinner once in a while. I have seen what you men eat when you cook for yourselves." She knew about Susan but she didn't mention her directly, and David was glad. Talking about her death made people uncomfortable, and he preferred avoiding it. Four years had pretty much numbed the pain, but not the lingering anger that had replaced it. David couldn't say he had looked forward to getting older, to getting short of breath and lame, but if he was to be lucky enough to have a long life, he had wanted Susan to share it, and without her he felt cheated.

"We're glad you've moved up here," Mrs. Ponder said changing the subject, "and you have a nice place there by the river."

"I was lucky to get it," David said.

"Can't talk you into doctoring some, can we?" Dub asked, hopefully. "Henson could use a good doctor."

David had heard that a lot in the two years since he moving to Henson. It was a natural thing for people to think and even if it was selfish, it was innocent.

"No," said David. "Too many other things I want to do now. Besides, I have forgotten all the general medicine I ever knew and you don't need a cardiologist."

"There's an awful lot of heart trouble here," Dub said.

David smiled. They don't understand, he thought.

"Well," said Mrs. Ponder folding her napkin. "You two go on out in the living room and talk. I'll bring you some coffee." She stood up and began clearing the dishes.

"Here," David said pushing his chair back, "let me help you with that."

"Oh, no. Thank you, David," she said. "You two go on. I wouldn't want want to embarrass Dub."

Dub winked playfully at David. "Thanks, Momma," he said getting up and giving her a peck on the cheek. She feigned indifference. David followed Dub into the living room and sat on one of the worn leather sofas that faced each other in front of the stone fireplace. Dub put a pine log on the coals, stirred them with a poker and watched as the fire snapped to life.

"Tell me more about Lomax," David said. Dub sat on the sofa opposite him.

"Well," Dub laughed, "there's been a lot of fellows like him come through here." He took a cigar from his pocket, peeled off the cellophane wrapper and thoroughly lit the cigar with a kitchen match, rolling the cigar slowly in the flame as he puffed. Then, inspecting the end to satisfy himself that it was lit, he leaned back in the sofa, crossed his legs and blew a smoky plume at the ceiling.

"Typical Texan, if you ask me," Dub continued, as if there had been no interruption. "Big butter-and-egg man. Thinks he's gonna make a killing on that mine. But he doesn't know any more about mining than pigs know about singing." It was one of Dub's favorite expressions.

"Lomax is really running it?"

"He is," Dub confirmed around the cigar. From the tone of his voice it was clear Dub didn't think much of Lomax. "Oh, he hired some hotshot mining engineers to come in and look it over. They spent three days up there poking around. I guess they told Lomax it was a good deal, but he'll learn."

"You think he made a mistake?"

"Oh, he'll do okay for now," Dub said, "but it's pockety ore. Always was. Big payloads for a while and then nothing. The vein is all broken up. Scattered all through the mountain. Hard to tell where it's going to lead ." Dub leaned forward and brushed something off the toe of his boot. "And it's rebellious."

"Rebellious?"

"It's what they call rebellious ore. Tellurium. Combination of sulphur and gold and silver. A lot of the ore around here is like that. But she was a rich mine once. It made this town. Changed it from a mining camp to a boom town. First year they shipped ninety wagon loads of ore. Some of it so pure they didn't even have to sort it."

Dub shifted his weight and settled back into a more comfortable spot in the sofa. "Actually," he went on, "mining was late coming to the valley. The first strikes in Colorado were over at Clear Creek. At Central City. A couple of guys who had done some mining in Georgia found some placer gold in the creek, color they called it in those days, and followed it back upstream to the mother lode forty miles up the canyon. Then it began to spread this way but the Indians kept the mining out of here 'till 1873. That's the year the Brunot Treaty was signed."

"The Indians got the short end of that deal," David said.

"Sure did," Dub puffed. "Lost all their land. They sold four million acres for an allowance of $25,000 a year. At first, you know, the Indians only wanted to sell the mountain tops." Dub paused, eyebrows raised, and looked at David to see if he understood. Satisfied, he went on. "It seemed logical to the Indians. The miners wanted to get at the high country where the ore was. So the Indians said they could have the mountain tops if they would stay out of the hunting grounds in the valleys and if they would agree not to build any houses and be out of the country every year by fall."

"Probably wouldn't have worked," David suggested.

"Course not," Dub agreed. "So the Indians ended up losing the whole thing. The mountains and the valleys. Ended up in Utah." Dub leaned forward and expertly rolled the ash off his cigar into an ashtray on the table between the sofas. He leaned back, elbow on the arm of the sofa, holding the cigar in his raised hand. "The first mining in this part of the state was over at Silverdale," Dub continued. "It was called Baker's Park then. Baker was quite an operator. Probably more interested in developing the area than in mining. He spread stories about the gold to get people to move in over his toll road and buy his land."

"I heard that was some road," David said.

"They tried taking wagons in but it was too steep. And too rough. The teamsters said it was mostly holes two feet deep with a stump in each hole. Walking in was the only way. Had to leave the wagons at Wagon Wheel Gap and go on the rest of the way with burros. That's why Meers built his toll road. From Saguache over Alpine Pass to the diggings at Silverdale. There was nothing here in the valley then. His road was good enough for wagons. It opened up this whole country." He paused, reflecting, puffing rhythmically on the cigar he held between his finger and his thumb.

"Another developer," David added.

"Right. Meers was doing the same thing Baker was trying to do. Charge toll to the miners then haul in the goods they needed and sell 'em those too. It was workers on Meers' road that found the Golden Fleece mine."

"The first mine in the valley."

"Oh, there was some blast-and-pray holes but the Golden Fleece was the first real mine. In the beginning the ore was right on the surface. But that played out pretty quick. Then it was hard rock mining. It wasn't poor man's mining like California where a man with little or no equipment could make a fortune. No pan-and-sluce operations here. Hard rock mining was tough and expensive. Lotsa' capital required. A tunnel forty feet deep was about as far as a man could go without outside help. What most of the men hoped for was to find a good claim and sell it for a big price."

"Like the oil wildcatters."

"Exactly," said Dub. "That's what happened with the Golden Fleece. Someone would work it for a while and then sell it. It was a chancy business. One fellow got down to his last stick of dynamite and when he set it off the blast opened up a pocket of ore worth ten thousand dollars. The previous owner had given up ten feet from one of the main ore bodies."

"Ten thousand dollars with one blast," David said, quietly.

"Rich ore in that mine. The same as the ore over at Leadville. That's what gave rise to the idea of the Great San Juan gold belt. They thought it ran all the way from Leadville to here."

"And they swarmed in looking for it," David said.

"And some of the places they went." Dub shook his head slowly in disbelief. "One canyon was so steep they couldn't find a flat place to sleep, so they drove stakes in the ground and rolled a log down against the stakes and slept with their feet braced on the log, nearly standing straight up."

Dub's wife appeared carrying a tray with a pot of coffee and two heavy mugs. The men leaned forward expectantly as she set it on the table between them. "There," she said.

"Thanks, Momma," Dub said.

"Won't you join us?" David asked.

"Sounds too much like man talk to me," she replied, taking a foil wrapped square from her apron pocket and placing it on the table in front of David. "For your breakfast."

"Thank you," David said. "And thanks again for the supper."

"My pleasure," she said graciously. "You must come again. She smiled, said good night and walked back to the kitchen.

Dub filled David's cup and then his and leaned back in the sofa, coffee cup in one hand, cigar in the other.

"You know," he took a noisy sip, "some of those miners were real characters . One fellow, 'ol Ben Tilton, brought a mule over Alpine Pass one winter on snow shoes he had taught the animal to wear." Dub laughed softly to himself. "Later that same year he blew his arm off when he drilled into a missed hole."

"A missed hole?" David asked over his cup.

"The blasting holes were drilled into the tunnel walls with a hammer and drill, an iron rod with a chisel bit on the end." He pronounced iron as if it were spelled a-r-n. "They pounded the drill with a four pound hammer, turning the drill between each blow. Then they filled the hole with dynamite. Well," he took another sip, "sometimes all the charges didn't explode and after the blasting it was hard to know just where the live charges were, especially if your partner had put some of the charges in. Well, ol' Tilton somehow pounded his drill into one of those live holes and it blew his arm off."

"It's a wonder it didn't kill him," David said.

"Probably would have if he hadn't cauterized it."

"Probably would have bled to death," said David.

"Mmmm," Dub said swallowing. "But he mined for years after that. And for a while he was sheriff of Henson. Even though he only had one arm he always wore two guns and kept his aim sharp shooting out the letters on the wooden grave markers in the Lone Tree Cemetery. He was killed in a snow slide over on Palmetto Gulch. His mining partner came back from town one day and saw the avalanche track near the cabin. He found Ben's hat on the snow and followed the slide down to where he spotted Ben's hand sticking up out of the snow. He dug down and found ol' Ben's body, standing straight up, frozen stiff, that one arm extended out in front of him like he was stopping traffic." For emphasis Dub mimed the one armed gesture.

"Rough times, Doc," Dub said. "Lots of men got killed. Froze to death. Caved in on. Blown up."

"Were these men who had come back to Colorado after giving California a try?" David asked.

"Some of them, but they came from everywhere. Half of 'em weren't even Americans. Came from all over Europe. English. Austrians. Italians. Cousin Jacks."

"Cousin Jacks?"

"Cornish," Dub explained. "They grew up mining coal. Came over to work the coal mines in Nova Scotia. Then migrated out to Michigan and Montana. Butte. Then they came down here." Dub leaned forward and poured himself another cup. "More coffee?" he motioned to David, offering the pot.

"Thanks." David slid his cup over and Dub filled it.

"There were lots of Italians too."

"Here in Henson?"

"Lots of 'em. Especially at the Hidden Treasure. At one time there was sixty of 'em working there. One year they went on strike. The owners had passed a rule that all the men had to eat their meals at the company commissary. That was too much. The governor sent in four companies of militia on a train. They met up with another train at Gunther where they picked up the Italian Consulate."

David raised his eyebrows. Where does he get these stories, he thought.

"There were rumors that the track into Henson was mined," Dub continued, "so a locomotive went ahead of the train, real slow, but nothing happened. When they got to town the Consul sent a message up to the miners from the Italian king himself, ordering the men to meet with the militia. Then he rode up the canyon to the mine alone in a buggy with a white handkerchief tied to the buggy whip. It was snowing hard. When he got to the mine, the men were all gathered to meet him. Most of 'em had guns. It was a tense situation. For a minute the Consul sat looking out over the crowd. It was real quiet. Then he stood up to his full height and threw open his overcoat. Under it he was wearing full-dress tails and across his chest was a green, white and red sash. The miners cheered. "

"Classy," said David. "What happened then?"

"Well, he talked them into surrendering and they all walked back down to Henson. Ten miles in a snow storm, in a single file line following the Consul in the buggy."

David tried to picture the scene. The Consul sitting erect in the buggy, the white handkerchief fluttering in the wind, the line of solemn black figures in the snow.

Dub puffed at the cigar, realized that it had gone out, and put it in the ashtray. "The next day," he said, as if just remembering that he hadn't finished, "the mine owners announced that in the future they wouldn't hire any more Italians and they gave the miners thirty days to get out of the country."

"Good deal," David said, sarcastically.

"That's the way they were sometimes," Dub commented cooly.

"So the miners who came in here eventually ended up working for the big mining companies?"

"Most of 'em. Some of 'em left but most stayed for the money. Shift work for two dollars a day."

Ironic, thought David. They came to the wilderness alone as free spirits, individualists, and ended up doing day labor for a big company. The adventurers became captives, the entrepreneurs became employees.

"Why did the mines shut down?" David asked. "Did the ore just play out?"

"Well, yes and no," Dub replied. "Mostly it was the price of the ore. In the 1870's the government quit minting silver so the mines around here shifted to gold. There was plenty of gold, but it was hard to recover. They brought in stamp mills and smelters but the gold was bound up with other elements and smelting wouldn't separate it. At one point the Golden Fleece was sending its ore all the way to Swansea in Wales to be processed."

"That must have been expensive," David said.

"And that's what got 'em. You take the Golden Fleece." Dub re-lit his cigar. "In its lifetime the Golden Fleece produced over eight million dollars in gold and silver ore but they couldn't make a profit. Just before World War I, they walked off and left it."

"Walked off?"

"Well, the final thing was the water. They couldn't handle it. One of the main tunnels flooded and that did it. Rumors were they left twenty sacks of high grade ore in that flooded tunnel. That was in 1917. They never came back. In 1943, an English company bought it for back taxes."

"And now Lomax is giving it a try. How's he doing?"

"Hard to tell," said Dub. "He's such a windbag. But the gold is still there. Providence hid the gold so one generation couldn't find it all. Who knows, maybe Lomax will get lucky. And," Dub's eyes sparkled, "there is one interesting thing."

"What's that?"

"It may be just coincidence," he said with a wry smile, "but one of the first things Lomax brought in was a water pump."

The two men talked for hours, David gently prodding Dub for stories and Dub gladly telling them, both men, if only for a while, recreating their pasts. Their relationship had begun with stories told around stoves and by fireplaces and on sunny afternoon porches. Stories that made a young boy dream and imagine and pretend, made him marvel at the lives men led, ponder what drove them so. Stories with heros and hardships, stories with heartache and hallelu-jahs, stories of boom and bust and of loving and dying and stories that made room for nostalgia, made wonder unashamed and nurtured in his greening consciousness a reverence for this land of space and light.

At midnight, David turned down a third cup of coffee, thanked Dub again for supper and left. Driving home, he found thought about the men who had spent themselves on the niggardly mountains, and marveled again at their inextinguishable optimism and hope, their loneliness and pride.

When he got to his cabin he sat for a while looking at a book of photographs taken during the mining boom days. Pictured there in black and white, shadows secured, were the men who came to pit themselves against the mountains. There were the dreamers, the drifters, the hopeful and the hopeless. In pairs and in large groups, from mine dumps and tent cities and tram cars, they looked solemnly out across the years. All had beards or mustaches or goatees. All wore hats. Some had vests. Something in their dark, earnest eyes reminded David of the eyes of immigrants lining the rails of great ships, eyes that looked back with a singular mixture of longing and sadness, apprehension and resignation and hope.

David got up and went outside and sat in the cool darkness of the porch. For a while he watched the moon as it made its way toward the mountain. Then he closed his eyes and from somewhere in the still distance he could hear, as if it were real, the measured rhythmic song of hammer and drill.

11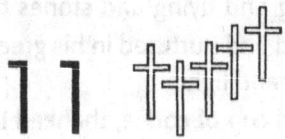

Rutherford B. Hayes was President of the United States in 1877, Henson, Colorado was the Queen City of the San Juan and Alfie Hammit had been on the run for three years. In September of that same year work was completed on the Henson County courthouse.

Two full stories high and sixty feet long, the sturdy courthouse was the largest building in Henson and except for the Presbyterian church, the only one which was white. Neither granite nor Gothic but none-the-less businesslike, it stood on a double lot at the corner of Second Street and Gunther Avenue facing the Orient, the birthplace of justice, shoulders square, arms folded, feet firmly planted as if it had come to stay, a steadfast white magistrate among the rough-cut boom-town transience of the little brown town.

During its long term the durable old courthouse had been the official community headquarters not only for local government business, but also for varied day-to day civic affairs, commonplace and grand. It was archives and auditorium, jailhouse and playhouse, assembly hall and ballroom. It was there births were registered, taxes flied, disputes settled. It was there Shakespeare was played out. It was there campaigns were waged. It was there that Prohibition was praised. And it was there one August afternoon in 1884 that Alfred G. Hammit, the Cannibal of Colorado, was sentenced to hang by the neck until he was dead.

David parked on the street and walked to the door at the rear of the courthouse. Forty years before David and his seven-year old brother had walked up these same steps and through the same door to file the claim on their mine. The abandoned mine the two boys were claiming was on a hill just across the river from Dub Ponder's dude ranch. David had discovered the old mine the first year he had been allowed to ride a horse alone and every summer after that when his family had come on vacation, David and his brother, pretending they were prospectors, had used the old mine as their playground.

Each morning the two boys had packed their lunches in the saddlebags and rode off to the mine, careful to cross the river at a different place each time to confuse any claim jumpers who might be following them. All day the two little prospectors scooped the yellow dirt that passed for gold ore into empty cotton sugar sacks and carefully hid them away. There were no buildings around the old mine site and the tunnel had caved in a safe distance beyond the entrance, but to David and his brother the wealth of that mine was as real as any pirate treasure trove.

It had been Dub's idea for the boys to officially claim the mine. He had even driven them to the courthouse to check the claim patent records. Colorado mining law specified that, to keep a claim active, the owner had to make at least a hundred dollars in improvements each year and if he did not the property could be reclaimed. According to the register no improvements had been made on the boy's playground mine since 1898. So, on a fine July afternoon in 1948 the Texan Lode and all pertaining mineral rights, had become the sole property of Misters David and Harry Walton.

David couldn't help thinking about that day as he entered the courthouse and headed down the hall to the County Clerk's office. Miss Hartman was no longer the Clerk. Another woman had taken her place. David didn't ask her about the Texan Lode .

"Good morning," David said to the woman. How are you today?" He was trying to be charming, worried that, even though he had seen the transcript of the Hammit trial before, somehow, something might have changed and this woman might now be able to refuse to let him see the court records.

"Good morning," she said, briskly. "What can I do for you". She was an small alert woman, with round bright eyes. She was wearing a brown tweed jacket and an orange sweater vest. As she waited for David to reply, she looked at him quizzically, moving her head in short, quick expectant jerks.

Like a robin, David thought. "I wonder if it might be possible for me to take a look at the transcript of some of the court proceedings?"

"Of course," she chirped. "You must mean the Hammit trial?"
David relaxed.

"Oh, yes mam, if I could. How'd you know that?"

"That's the only court records anyone around here ever wants to see," she said "They've nearly worn them out. Come with me," she said, hopping up from behind the desk. David followed obediently.

There was no one else in the building and the irregular cadence of their footsteps echoed in the empty wooden hallway. The clerk stopped at a paneled door, unlocked it easily and led David into a small library. It was a spare functional room with one double-hung window and no frills. In the center of the floor and covering the largest part of it was a plain rectangular table of dark wood and drawn up to it, four worn matching chairs. The two side walls were lined ceiling to floor with shelves filled with identical leather-backed volumes. It was a room intended for serious work.

The clerk walked directly to the end of the third shelf on the right hand wall and using both little hands, slipped one of the heavy books from the shelf and held it out to David.

"It starts on page 1126," she said, very businesslike. "You're welcome to use this room. We close for an hour at noon, otherwise the hours are from nine to five, Monday through Friday."

David, relieved, took the book and held it out before him. As far as he knew, this was the only transcript of the Hammit trial. Without it, he and Fuller would never be able to reconstruct the story.

"Is there anything else I can get for you?" she blinked.

"No. Thank you very much." She turned to leave.

"Actually, there is one thing," David said, hesitantly, afraid to push his luck too far.

"Yes," she said, turning back toward him, blinking in anticipation.

"Is the courtroom open?"

"Yes," she said. "It's on the second floor. The stairs are just across from my office."

"Thank you," said David. "You have been very helpful."

"Make yourself at home." She smiled and left in one motion.

Still holding the book, David waited until she was gone. Then he turned, put the book on the table and stood looking down at it. The gray cloth cover was worn and stained and the corners were rounded with use. He lifted the cover reverently. In the center of the first page, Records of Henson County Court, June 1, 1884 - December 31, 1884 was written in elegant, black scrip. He turned the crisp blue-lined page to the inventory where, line by line, in chronological order, the trials were listed with dates and page numbers. The Hammit entry was easy to find. It was on the second page of the inventory. August 20 1884. pp. 1126-1294.

He pulled out a chair and sat down facing the book, opening it carefully to the first page of the Hammit proceedings. There, in the same ink, the handwritten record began.

August 20, 1884. Alfred G. Hammit vs the State of Colorado.

David took a deep breath and began to read. He read slowly, making notes, resisting the temptation to race ahead, to look for clarification of points he was particularly interested in. He was aware of that intellectual trap in research and was trying to be objective. He had done enough research to know that the researcher often brought with him a point of view, an unconscious bias, sometimes even an hypothesis, and that with this mind-set was easily mislead. Often it was comfortably easy to find evidence to support pre-conceived notions. It was much more trying to consider all the evidence, account for all the variables, find answers for all questions, even the disruptive ones.

The stylized handwriting was difficult to read. The sloping letters were neat and carefully spaced, written by someone accustomed to writing, but with a flair that only slowly became familiar. Unlike many of the other old handwritten documents David had seen, there were periods at the ends of the sentences, but o's and a's were difficult to distinguish, as were m's and n's. Terminal t's were not crossed and the transcriber used the archaic double s.

He read for a hour and a half and then, trying to pace himself, walked over to the drugstore for a cup of coffee. He had hoped to see Fuller to tell him he had found the transcript, but decided against interrupting him. They could talk at noon. When he returned to the courthouse, he first went upstairs to look at the courtroom where the trial had taken place.

The door opened into the rear of the empty gallery, five rows of chairs arranged with military precision on either side of a center aisle. Beyond the chairs, crossing the room from side to side a walnut banister divided the room into two nearly equal halves. David slowly walked to the banister and looked into the partitioned space.

A row of captain's chairs, their backs against the banister, faced the three large windows in the front wall of the building. Under the center window was a plain wooden table, one chair behind it, another drawn up to the end and turned to face the gallery. A brass lamp suspended from the high pressed-tin ceiling hung over the center of the table. Against the right-hand wall near the wood stove, twelve more chairs were arranged in two rows of six.

Glancing back quickly to make sure he had closed the gallery door behind him, David walked through the passage in the banister to the witness chair at the end of the table. For half an hour he sat looking out over the empty gallery, trying to visualize the scene in the crowded courtroom, trying to picture the faces, trying to imagine what it must have been like for the forty-two year old Hammit during those four August days.

If Alfie Hammit's luck was bad, his judgment had been worse. According to his testimony at the trial his childhood was not a happy one. When he was seven his mother died. After her death Alfie was at the mercy of his father who believed beatings would stop the seizures. At sixteen he left home, lied about his age and his epilepsy, and joined the army at Dingman's Ferry, Pennsylvania. Within two months he was mustered out when he had a seizure in the mess hall. From Pennsylvania he went to Iowa where he enlisted in Company F, 16th U.S. Infantry. Two months later he was give a medical discharge.

Angry and alone he drifted through the West for twenty years trying to find his place, living a life not so much of dishonesty as make-believe. He tried to cope with the unpleasantness of life by denying it. Truth was what he said it was, a way of making things over.

He worked as a teamster, a hunter, a guide and finally as a hard rock miner where he nearly lost his hand. He tried prospecting but failed and in Salt Lake City, down to his last twenty dollars, he learned of the gold strike in Colorado. Desperate for one more chance at "the golden fleece," he lied again, passing himself of as an experienced guide and joined a group of men headed for Breckenridge, a journey only he would complete.

When he had first been accused of the murders he said he lied because he was afraid. He said he had escaped from jail because he was afraid. He said he hid out in Wyoming because he was afraid and after ten years, just when he thought everyone had forgotten, there, in Wyoming's permissive anonymity a thousand miles from Henson and against all odds, he met one who remembered.

"Oh, there you are." The voice startled him. The clerk was framed in the doorway at the rear of the room. "I'm afraid I have to lock up now."

David got up quickly and walked self-consciously toward the woman who closed the door behind them and followed him down the stairs.

"We open again at one o'clock," she reminded him.

Right," said David avoiding her eyes. "Right. I'll come back at one." He left without looking back, walked quickly down the steps and started across the street to the Pine Cone. When he walked in, Fuller was waiting.

"It's still there," David said as he sat down. "I was worried I might not get to see it."

"You get much done?"

"Just a start," David replied. He didn't tell Fuller about the courtroom incident. "How about you?"

"They're all there," Fuller said. "Every issue of the *Silver World* since Number 1 September 20, 1874. It took me most of the morning to locate the 1884 issues. Thank goodness they are not on microfilm. That blinds me."

"I know what you mean," David agreed, squinting. He had spent hours at the microfilm readers working on the Hawthorne project. "It's kinda' fun being back at work, isn't it?"

"In a way," said Fuller. "It is interfering with fishing though."

"Tomorrow," David said. "We'll take a day off."

"Now that's my kind of job," said Fuller. "One day on, one day off." David laughed. He knew Fuller was joking. The Hawthorne book project had proved how productive Fuller could be.

Dallas brought their lunch and while they ate the two men passed an hour talking about what they had learned that morning. Having access to the original sources—the transcript of the trial and the newspaper accounts—David and Fuller would be able to avoid some of the error that inevitably creeps into research based on second-hand accounts. Misconceptions and misinterpretations passed on, sometimes innocently, sometimes reverently, from one authority to another, especially those disinclined to field research, and tended to sanctify the same faulted conclusions.

David found getting to the bottom of things irresistible. For him, historical research was like medical research. He enjoyed the search for clues, observing variations from the expected, cross-checking, confirming, then synthesizing the data into a thesis. It was the sort of deductive reasoning his medical training had prepared him for. It was mystery solving, like making a diagnosis in a sick patient.

"Well," David said finishing his coffee, "time to get back at it.

Come by my place after you finish at the newspaper. I'll pick up some barbecue at Bud's. We can compare notes."

"You just finished eating and you're already thinking about food?" Fuller said, feigning amazement.

"A man's got to plan ahead," David said. "See you at five."

"Good enough. No pickles. Extra sauce."

12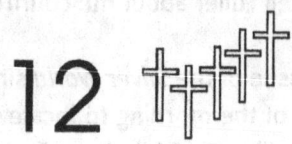

The silver and blue plane banked hard around the bare shoulder of Shavano Peak, leveled off and dived at the runway. Through the oval window at his elbow, Ed Lomax could see the pasture land along the river, a narrow green strip between the sage hills of the Gunther River valley. To the south the elk-colored hills rose one behind the other up the stepped terrace of the Alpine Plateau to the blue bulk of the San Juan mountains fifty miles away.

Just over the apron of the runway the pilot flared the little plane and slammed it down hard onto the tarmac, bounced it once and then dropped the nose and and began the noisy roll out.

"Ex-Navy," Lomax said disparagingly. "They never get over landing on carriers." Neither he nor the man beside him had spoken on the forty-minute flight from Denver. Reluctant to get involved in a conversation with a stranger, both men had busied themselves reading, but now as the aircraft rolled toward the terminal a natural conclusion was only moments away and they began to talk.

"Were you in the Navy?" the stranger asked politely.

"No," said Lomax. "Air Force. But I can tell a swabbie pilot by the way he lands." He closed the book he had been reading and tucked it into the zipper bag he took from under the seat. Books were better protection than magazines against talkative airplane seat mates. People were more reluctant to interrupt a serious book reader. "Were you in the service?" Lomax asked, turning to look at the middle-aged stranger. He wore a white western shirt with pearl snaps. Except for a tell-tale hat line across the forehead, his face had the ruddy tan of an outdoor worker. A rancher, Lomax thought.

"Marines," the stranger said.

"A jarhead!" Lomax laughed. "Well, you know all about swabbies then."

The man smiled. "I do," he said.

The plane rolled to a near stop in front of the terminal. The starboard engine roared briefly pushing the plane around in a tight quarter turn then abruptly shut down. The passengers unbuckled their seat belts, gathered their things and stood to wait passively in the aisle while the stewardess opened the door and lowered the steps. In the doorway of the cockpit, the young pilot stood smiling and thanking the passengers as they filed past.

"Great job, Commander," Lomax said sarcastically as he approached the pilot. "Are you going to log both of those landings?" Lomax laughed. "A good landing is one you can walk away from, right?" he added over his shoulder as he ducked out the door. The pilot only stared, coldly. The rancher lowered his head, avoiding the pilot's eyes, and hurried out the door.

Lomax walked across the tarmac, through the terminal and out to the long-term parking lot where he had left the jeep while in Texas. Parking it was much less trouble than leaving the jeep in Henson and trying to arrange for rides.

Driving out of the parking lot Lomax turned onto the highway and headed west. He had planned his trip carefully. First he would drive to his house, park the jeep in the garage and go to bed without using any lights. The next day was Friday, the day Sonny would take the ore shipment to Salt Lake. While Sonny was gone Lomax would go up to the mine and check things out for himself. Then he would know for sure if Sonny was stealing from him.

Three miles beyond Gunther Lomax slowed at the intersection to let an oncoming car pass, then turned south toward Henson.The sun had set behind the high blue ridge. The sky just over the mountains was pale and clear except for one long cloud bank as soft and gray as lint. In an hour it would be dark.

For the first several months of the operation receipts from the mine had been better than Lomax had expected. Finding the bags of ore left behind in the flooded tunnel had been helpful but even after that the vein in Number Three tunnel had paid off well. Lomax had never actually intended to develop the mine. He only wanted to produce enough ore to pump up his cash flow and establish a record of good yield at the smelter so he could sell the property at a profit. At least that was his plan. But the ore proved to be richer than he thought and for the first nine months it had averaged four hundred dollars a ton.

Then receipts began to drop off. Only slightly at first then more each month. The checks from the smelter still came regularly but each month they were less. Sonny was working. Lomax made sure of that. He had gone to Henson several times to check on him. Records from the smelter indicated that the weight of the ore delivered to the smelter each trip was about the same but the quality seemed less, as if the vein were petering out. That would not be a good sign for potential buyers.

Lomax had called his mining engineer, who seemed surprised and said it was unusual for the yield from a mine like the Golden Fleece to change slowly. The mine's ore, volcanic magma which had seeped in between the layers of broken rock and hardened into mineral-rich veins, was deposited in pockets of almost uniform quality. When the pocket was mined out, the ore was gone, but the change would not likely be gradual. The engineer offered to survey the mine again but Lomax had decided to wait.

It should have occurred to him then Lomax recalled but it didn't. Maybe he was just too busy. Maybe confusion over the oil rig deals had distracted him. Whatever it was there was no excuse and as he drove along the dark road, he cursed his own stupidity .

Doubtless he would have caught on sooner or later but it might have been several months and thousands of dollars later if it were not for that night at the Houston Petroleum Club. At a fund raiser for a local politician, Lomax had overheard his friend Bill Moncrief describing how he had caught one of his wild-catters stealing oil from a storage tank at one of his wells. Moncrief said he had suspected it for months before he actually caught the man at it one night. As Lomax listened to the story it had become clear why the receipts had been dropping. Sonny was high-grading him. A practice as old as mining itself.

Within a week Lomax was headed to Henson. He was going to see for himself if Sonny was stealing from him and if so, this time, Sonny was going to jail.

*   *   *

Sonny had been in Henson all day, waiting all morning for the parts for his truck to arrive from Gunther,and then all afternoon for the lethargic mechanic to get around to replacing the spent alternator. He had tried hard to be patient. Vernon was the only mechanic in Henson and Sonny didn't want to antagonize him more than he already seemed to be.

While he waited Sonny had gone to the grocery store, checked for his mail at the post office—nothing from Lomax—and even taken a walk along the river and for a while, watched two men fishing below the bridge. Then at dark he returned to the car seat bench by the door of the AMOCO station to sit and wait and watch the clock over the Coke machine.

Bored and impatient he sat slouched in the splay of pale light. Moths drawn in from the night fluttered around the single bare bulb over the office doorway, their crippled shadows as if broken by the fall struggling on the textured surface of the gravel drive. From the open bay, he could hear the low croon of the radio and the intermittent, metallic tinkering of the mechanic

Lomax is such a jerk, he thought. He coulda' put me in the can, and instead he gives me the best job of my life. Man, is he stupid or what? He thinks he gettin' off cheap, but if that fat son-of-a-bitch knew I was clearing a thousand bucks a month selling off his rocks . . . . Sonny laughed to himself. Sure beats the hell out of breaking in houses. It's like finding money on the ground.

Sonny saw the headlights before he heard the motor. Bored with the waiting he watched with a detached indifference as the pair of white spots grew slowly larger, bringing with them through the darkness the familiar breathy whine of the jeep. The sound rose steadily in pitch until just before reaching the cattle guard it diminished abruptly as the jeep slowed and turned onto the road that led up the hill to Lomax's house.

Sonny, suddenly attentive, flipped away his cigarette and walked out beyond the light to the shoulder of the road. What the hell is he doing here, Sonny thought. He watched the jeep lights as they wound up the hill. Halfway to the house, the jeep lights went off. Sonny strained to see. Two minutes went by. No lights came on in the house. Ten minutes passed, still no lights. Then a quick chill swept through him. Not a chill of fear, but a chill of anger. That fat bastard is sneaking in, Sonny said under his breath. He's here to check on me!

Lomax had always written Sonny to tell him when he was coming. But not this time. That could mean only one thing. Lomax knows! Sonny thought. He walked quickly back to the service bay and looked in.

"How much longer?" he said to the mechanic, an edge on his voice. The mechanic was leaning over the fender of the pickup, his head under the hood.

Ten minutes," he replied without looking up.

Sonny lit a cigarette and walked back out to the bench. Lomax's house was still dark. Lomax doesn't want me to know he is in town. He'll be at the mine first thing in the morning. Well, damn good enough. This time I'll have a surprise for him.

Meeting David Walton had been good for Fuller. The year Fuller had spent at the alcohol rehabilitation center had restored his health but not his self-esteem. Moving to the cabin on Acme Creek was more of an escape than a manifestation of his independence. For months he had felt vulnerable and insecure and when David had contacted him about working on the Hawthorne project Fuller had been reluctant to take on the responsibility, or even a relationship. He was afraid, not just of failure but afraid that he simply would not be able to summon the energy to participate. Fuller had talked with his sister about David's offer and she had encouraged him to give it a try. He was glad he had. Writing the Hawthorne book had been therapeutic for Fuller, and he was thinking about his good luck as he drove down the Acme Creek road toward Henson.

He parked in front of the bank and climbed the covered stairway to the second floor office of the *Silver World*. The editor was sitting with his back to his desk and the door, looking out over the geraniums in the window box to the park across the street. He swiveled around in his chair when he heard Fuller.

"Back again?" he asked. Tod Lumis was the fifth editor in the hundred-and-fifteen year history of the little newspaper. He had bought it when he moved to Henson after the war and during that time he had written most of the articles, done the photography, sold the ads, made the lay-outs and even delivered them each week to the printer in Salida. What had started as a hobby had become a full time job.

"Going right at it," Fuller said. "I appreciate your letting me work here like this. I hope I'm not getting in your way"

"Not at all," Lumis responded quickly. "Are you finding what you need?"

"I'm finding that the people of Henson wanted to see Alfred Hammit hang," said Fuller.

"The paper was pretty rough on him, wasn't it?" Lumis said. "I remember looking through some of those old issues when I first moved up here. Quite a story"

"Well, it was a sensational trial, wasn't it?"

Lumis agreed. "By the way," he added, apologetically. "I have to leave town tomorrow. I'll be away for a few days . . . ."

"Oh?" Fuller tried not to let his disappointment show. He had warmed quickly to the details of the Hammit trial and now, charmed by the familiar, seductive momentum of the research, he was reluctant to be interrupted.

"But," Lumis continued, "I'll leave a key next door with Mary. Feel free to come and go as you like."

Fuller's disappointment had showed and Lumis could see the relief in Fuller's smile.

"I should be finished in a few days, maybe by the time you get back."

"Look," Lumis said, his outstretched hand making a slow-down gesture, "don't rush. Take your time. I'm glad that after all these years those old papers are getting some use. Frankly," he paused just long enough for a slight resigned smile, "I'm envious of you two. If I hadn't been so busy with the paper . . . ."

Lumis didn't finish the sentence. It wasn't necessary.

Fuller worked in the file room through the day, leaving only once to meet David for lunch. For three more hours he poured over the stacks of yellowed newspapers, carefully unfolding and re-folding the brittle sheets as he worked. At four thirty, when he paused to stretch his back, he looked at his watch for the first time since noon. He was surprised at the energy these projects with David seemed to have given him. By the time he arrived at David's cabin he was more animated than usual.

"Listen to these headlines," Fuller said to David. Human Jerked Beef. The Man Who Lived on Meat Cut From His Murdered Chums. A Cannibal Who Gnaws on The Choice Cuts of His Fellow Man. The Fiend Who Became Corpulent Upon a Diet of Human Steak."

"The poor guy didn't have a chance," replied David.

"What an onslaught!" said Fuller. "Day after day of the same stuff." He turned through the notes he had made. "Here's my favorite." Fuller read: "Today Alfred Hammit, that poisonous reptile with villainous and ugly visage was locked away in the Henson County jail. The confirmed vagabond, with small sunken eyes and a savage moustache, displayed a sullen and defiant air as Sheriff Campbell led this murderous fiend and ghoul to the cell where he would await his fate. The next chapter in this sordid tale will be the conviction of this monster and the last chapter will be his deserved death on the gallows."

He dropped the papers to his lap. "That was before the trial started!" Fuller said, shaking his head with disbelief.

"Open and shut case," David added sarcastically.

"And that was an editorial! The so-called news stories were even worse. One after another accused Hammit of a whole series of unsolved crimes all over the West. He was said to have murdered his mining partner in Montana and then stole his horse and money. They said he killed a second mining partner in Idaho, and wounded a third. While trapping in Utah he was said to have robbed and killed yet another partner stealing two thousand dollars worth of furs. Then in Wyoming he murdered and robbed a traveler. Back in Salt Lake City he was jailed for robbery and counterfeiting."

"He was quite a busy boy," David observed. "You suppose any of that is true?"

"It's hard to believe he could have gotten by with all of that," Fuller replied. "Most of it seems to be unsubstantiated rumor." Fuller leafed through his notes, then closed his notebook

"Any response from Hammit?"

"No direct quotes but there was one thing." Fuller frowned, remembering. "Just before the trial the newspaper published a copy of Hammit's so-called confession which the paper claimed was made at the Los Pinos Agency just after he was arrested."

"In April?"

"Actually May 4th, according to the story. Apparently the confession wasn't signed by Hammit or anyone else for that matter but it was said to have been recorded by a Hans Laufer." Fuller looked up at David. "Ever heard that name?"

"It's in the trial records. Laufer was one of the witnesses. For the prosecution, I think"

"The confession was written in the third person, supposedly as Hammit told it. According to Laufer Hammit said he returned to camp one night to discover that while he was out hunting four of the men had killed Swan, the oldest in the party. They had eaten the flesh from his legs and breasts and divided his money. Two days later Miller was killed with a hatchet as he stooped over to pick up a piece of firewood. The killer's identity wasn't given. Hammit said Miller had been chosen by the group because he was fat. Next Humphreys and Noon were killed leaving only Hammit and Bell. After traveling several more days Bell tried to kill Hammit by clubbing him with a rifle but the stock broke against a tree. In the struggle that followed Hammit said he killed Bell with a hatchet and lived off his body till he got to the Indian Agency at Los Pinos."

"That version came out at the trial, too," David said.

"But it can't be right," Fuller protested. "All five of the bodies were found together in one place. At the same campsite."

"Right, but remember," David said, "at the time of that confession, the bodies hadn't been found."

"Oh, right," Fuller remembered. "What did you mean that version?

"At the trial two different versions of the story came out ," David said. "The first version was related by a man named McNutt, the first witness called by the prosecution. He told the same story you read in the newspaper, the confession attributed to Hammit. McNutt was in the original party of twenty-five men who had started out from Utah. He was one of the larger group who stayed behind in Ouray's camp when Hammit and the other five left for Los Pinos. McNutt and his party left the Indian camp after Hammit's group, after the storm, and arrived at the Agency within a week. Apparently McNutt was still at the Agency when Hammit walked out of the mountains, three months later."

"According to McNutt's testimony," David continued, "when Hammit arrived at the Agency he had Miller's knife. When McNutt questioned him about it Hammit said Miller had stuck it in a tree and left it. McNutt said he was suspicious that Hammit was lying and organized a group to go back and look for the bodies. That's when Hammit made his confession."

"Probably Hammit told that story trying to discourage the search," Fuller said. "If they found the bodies all together and since Hammit was the only survivor, he would have certainly been arrested. By suggesting they had been killed in several different places, and by the other men, maybe he hoped that they would consider a search futile."

"Of course. The murderers were already dead, right?" David proposed.

"And Hammit only killed Bell in self defense," Fuller added.

"McNutt testified that Hammit told him that soon after leaving Ouray's camp they had become lost and after wandering in the mountains for several days, Swan had died. They ate his body and continued on. After four or five days Humphreys died and was eaten. Two days later when Hammit returned to camp from gathering wood, he found Miller dead. Then Bell shot Noon. It was at another campsite that Bell tried to kill Hammit with the rifle."

"Same story," Fuller said.

"Right."

"Did Hammit say why he didn't just shoot Bell?"

"No," replied David, "he didn't but McNutt couldn't resist taking a swipe at Hammit. He said Hammit admitted to him that he had grown fond of human flesh and he found the breasts of man the sweetest meat he had ever tasted."

"That must have wowed the jury," Fuller said. "Bro - ther!"

"McNutt said after the confession a search was organized."

"At McNutt's suggestion."

"Right," said David, "with Hammit as guide. McNutt said they went up Los Alamos Creek the way Hammit had walked out but every time they got near the crest of the mountains Hammit said he was lost. Finally they returned to the Agency. It was three months later that the bodies were found by a crew survey-ing for Meers' toll road from Saguache to Silverdale. That's when Hammit was arrested. McNutt said he was called over from Saguache to identify the bodies that had been found by the road crew. He said the bodies were pretty well decomposed and were lying only a few feet apart. He said all the skulls had been crushed. When questioned about it. McNutt was adamant that all five of the men's skulls were crushed."

"But . . . ."

"I know. That would have included Bell. McNutt also said it didn't appear the men had been camped in that spot for very long. There was only a small fire not completely burned."

"What could that mean?" Fuller mused.

"Hard to know. Either the men were killed just before Hammit walked out to the Agency or Hammit was camping somewhere else."

"Did he find anything at the campsite to corroborate Hammit's story? A hatchet? A rifle with a broken stock?"

"Nothing like that. Only some blanket fragments. What was left of the men's clothes. And a small blue box. McNutt said it was Hammit's medicine box but Hammit denied it."

"You said there were two versions of the story at the trial," Fuller said.

"That's right. After McNutt, the next witness called was a Colonel Adams. He had been the Indian Agent at Los Pinos when Hammit showed up. In the first part of his testimony Adams confirmed what McNutt had said. But the interest-ing part followed. After Hammit was arrested he was jailed in Saguache but he escaped. Ten years later he was arrested again in Wyoming, after a chance meeting with a man named Frenchy Carbazon who identified him. Carbazon knew Hammit from the Utah trip. He must have heard about the murders. He spotted Hammit at a bar near Fort Laramie and turned him in. The missing fingers?" David held up his hand and wiggled the last two fingers.

"What's the chance of that? All that space and so few people."

"Apparently there was still some question about Hammit's identity so Adams, who by that time was Post Office Inspector in Manitou Springs, was called to Denver to identify him. Hammit said he wanted to give his statement to Adams rather that the sheriff in Henson."

"From what I have read in the Henson newspaper, I can certainly understand that!" said Fuller.

"Adams said he telegraphed the sheriff, who agreed to let Adams take the statement. That statement—version two—was introduced as evidence and is recorded in the transcript of the trial. It began with Hammit detailing the rigors of the trip from Ouray's camp but the account of the deaths was quite different from the first version. According to this second statement, after they had been out fifteen or sixteen days, Hammit returned to camp one night to find all the men dead except Bell who jumped up and came at Hammit with a hatchet. Hammit said he shot Bell through the stomach then finished him off with the hatchet."

"No mention of the rifle?" Fuller said.

"No," replied David.

"Why did he change his story?"

"Well, according to Adams Hammit said that at the time of the first confession at Los Pinos he was excited and told the first story that came to his mind."

"And he couldn't tell the first version again after all the bodies were found in one place," Fuller said.

"Right."

"The evidence supports the second version doesn't it. But changing the story . . . that was bad."

"It gets more complicated," David went on. "When Hammit testified later in the trial he repeated this second version pretty much verbatim except for one thing."

"What's that?" Fuller asked.

"During the cross-examination, Hammit was asked again to describe Bell's murder. He re-told the story, the second version, saying that he shot Bell, who was coming at him with a hatchet. When asked where he shot Bell, Hammit pointed here."

Fuller, who had been looking at his notes while David talked, glanced up. David was pointing to his forehead, over his right eye.

"In the head! But . . . ."

"I know. Earlier he said he shot Bell in the stomach. Actually belly is the word he used."

"That doesn't seem to be the kind of thing you would forget," Fuller said suspiciously.

"Ummm," David agreed.

"That's worrisome," said Fuller taking his notes from his lap and placing them on the sofa beside him. "Now there are three versions. One, Hammit killed Bell with an axe. Two, he shot Bell in the abdomen. And three, he shot Bell in the head."

"Always in self defense."

"It's sounding more and more like Hammit killed them all."

"In their sleep?"

"Well, McNutt said all the men's skulls were crushed and all the bodies were found around a campfire. They were weak and starving," Fuller added when he saw David's expression.

"But so was Hammit," David argued. "How could he kill five men without waking any of them?"

"I don't know," said Fuller, "but not being straight about the details of Bell's death is awfully suspicious. If he had killed all five men as they slept the part about Bell's death would have been the part of the story he had to make up."

"And the easiest part to forget," David suggested.

"Exactly." Fuller got up and walked to the window where he stood for a moment thinking. Then he turned to face David. "What else did you learn?"

"Well, most of the trial focused on the murders but there was also quite a lot of discussion about the money."

"Money?"

"When Hammit showed up at the Indian Agency in Los Pinos he had Miller's knife and some money. Other members of the party who had stayed over at the Agency after they arrived from Ouray's camp thought it was strange that Hammit would have money since he was broke when he left Utah. When they questioned him about it Hammit said the only money he had was the $20 he brought with him from Utah, and $50 he got for the rifle he sold after he got to the Agency.

"That should be easy to confirm," said Fuller.

"That wasn't the problem," David said. "The big discussion was over a five hundred dollars Wells Fargo draft one of the men said Miller had with him when he left Ouray's camp. The prosecuting attorney spent a lot of time on that."

"If he could prove Hammit had robbed the men, it would have strengthened his motive for the murders."

"Exactly. Well," David leaned forward on his elbows smiling, "guess who was called to the stand next?"

Fuller shrugged.

"Otto Meers."

"Why?"

"Meers was living in Saguache when Hammit appeared at the Agency. Meers owned a store there. He testified that Hammit came to his store to buy shoes and clothes and that he, Meers, saw in the wallet Hammit produced, a blue Wells Fargo note. The blue notes were for five hundred dollars."

Fuller raised his eyebrows and his mouth formed a silent "Oh"

"But Hammit denied having it."

"Anyone else see it?" Fuller asked.

"Nope."

"So it's Meers' word against Hammit?"

"Right. Mr. Drifter Hammit against Mr. Otto Meers, who at the time of the trial just happened to be the owner of the newspaper and the toll road and the largest hotel in town and the only bank."

"But why would Meers lie about the money?"

"I'm not sure but he did have a motive, of sorts."

"What's that?"

"Well, Meers had a real interest in seeing Henson prosper. He owned most of the land there. Maybe he wanted Hammit convicted and hanged to show the world the strength of Henson's law and order. Who would move their family to an area where there was a cannibal on the loose?"

"M-a-a-ybe," Fuller conceded, reluctantly.

"And there is another reason Meers might have wanted to see Hammit hang," David added.

"What's that?"

"In Hammit's testimony he said when he made his first statement to Adams, Meers had been present. Afterwards, according to Hammit, Meers told him, 'You're a fool if you don't get out of here.'"

"He was right," said Fuller.

"Probably," David agreed. "They did put Hammit in jail. Right after they found the bodies."

"But then he escaped."

"Right," David said. "With help."

Fuller looked at David, surprised. "With help?"

"Hammit said that one night someone passed him a file and a key made from a knife blade."

"Did Hammit say who it was?"

"They asked him that at the trial."

"What did he say?"

"He pointed to Meers."

"Whoa!" Fuller exclaimed. "Aiding criminal escape? Why would he have taken a chance like that? No wonder he wanted Hammit convicted. This is getting complicated."

"It is, isn't it. Poor ol' Hammit. He didn't stand a chance. The circumstantial evidence was strong The county's most prominent citizen was testifying against him. No wonder he was convicted."

"And don't forget the newspaper," said Fuller, arms folded.

"You mean Meers' newspaper," corrected David.

"And in addition to the influence it had on the jurors, the paper whipped the town into a hanging frenzy after the trial. The sheriff was so afraid Hammit would be lynched he arranged for a secret night time transfer to the county jail in Gunther."

"The newspaper really helped convict him, didn't it?"

"No question. But there was one other thing I thought was strange. It was an editorial that appeared just after Hammit was convicted. The editor of the *Silver World* interviewed Hammit in jail and wrote that he found a man who appeared different from the one he had expected to see. He did not see—let's see here . . . ." Fuller walked over to the sofa and paged through his notes. "Oh, yes. Here it is." Fuller read: "I did not see that fiendish look. On the contrary he has a pleasant face and a mild gray eye that is not deep set and gleaming with hate. He is in fact a rather mild looking and mild mannered person."

Fuller looked up from the paper. "What do you make of that?"

"Conscience crisis?"

"Maybe," said Fuller. "Either that or after he was convicted it was safe to tell the truth.

"Villain or victim?" David said rhetorically. Then getting up from his chair he added, "That reminds me. I've got something I've been meaning to show you." He left the room and returned with a manila folder, opened it on the table in front of the sofa and sat down beside Fuller.

"Are you familiar with the dominant eye theory?" David asked.

"You mean in shooting?"

"No. For character analysis."

Fuller looked skeptical. "That's a new one. Try me." He leaned back and folded his arms across his chest in mock defiance.

"Well", David began, trying to be serious, "it goes like this. When you meet someone you naturally look at them predominantly with your right eye." He looked briefly at Fuller.

"Go on," Fuller challenged.

"Your right eye looks into their left eye."

"So." Fuller was smirking slightly.

Ignoring Fuller's skepticism, David continued, "So, as the theory goes we train our left eye to project the image we want to present to the public. But the unschooled right eye betrays our real character."

David resisted looking at Fuller, and went on. "If you place a sheet of paper over someone's photograph and look alternately at one half of the face and then the other you can see what I mean. Most faces are asymmetrical."

Fuller sat, smiling politely.

"And," David continued with emphasis, "if you cut the photograph and join the two left halves and the two right halves it is even more clear." He stopped and looked at Fuller. "You're wondering what the point is?"

"I think I know," Fuller said, leaning forward, elbows on his knees.

"Look at this," David said. "I made two copies of Hammit's picture and enlarged them on Dub's copy machine. Then I cut the photos down the center of his nose and taped two right halves and two left halves together."

"But one half is on the back side of the paper," Fuller objected

"Right, but If you hold them up to a bright light . . . ." David took one of the papers and held it up for Fuller to see. "This is a composite of the left halves of Hammit's face." He watched as Fuller studied the photo.

"Pretty rough looking character," Fuller said.

"Right," David agreed. "Now . . ." He took the other sheet and held it to the light. "Two right sides." The sad eyes spoke for themselves. "What do you think?"

"Interesting," Fuller said looking at the pictures. "But I don't think it would stand up in court, Walton." He took the other paper and held them both to the light, looking back and forth from one to the other then handed them back to David.

"So, you don't think Hammit was the villain he was cracked up to be," Fuller said.

"Do you?"

"I don't know."

David took the papers and put them in the folder. "Did you ever notice that in the old photographs no one was ever smiling?"

"No, "Fuller said with an indulgent smile.

"Think about it. All the pioneer families look defeated. Even the children. Here, for instance."

David took a book from the floor beside him, found the page he wanted and handed the open book to Fuller. Across the top of the page was a black-and-white photograph of a man and a woman and a small child, all posed obediently in front of their house of rough plank siding. From the looks of their clothes the family had turned out in their best things.

The young father was mustached and balding, his thin hair brushed down flat across his forehead. He wore the plain unbelted dungarees of a working man, a dark shirt buttoned at the collar and, perhaps borrowed for the photograph, perhaps even from the photographer, a three-buttoned suit coat with small lapels. His wife who appeared to be holding her breath, stood stiffly beside him, her black dress new and waisted so tightly and unnaturally that most of her stout frame seemed to have been displaced either upward into the over-sized bosom and mutton sleeves, or downward into the fullness of the broad unpleated skirt. An uneasy young boy obviously unaccustomed to the blousey white shirt and short pants stood at his mother's side leaning slightly against her leg. He held a tuck of her skirt in his small hand as if to moor himself against the unexpected. The piece was so set, the postures so rigid the subjects might have been standing, chins in place, behind lifesized cardboard cut-outs in a carnival midway tent.

The circumstances of the photograph are not clear. Perhaps they were on their way to church or to a party for the boy's fourth birthday, or perhaps the photographer was just passing through and the wife wanted—it would have been her idea—to have a family portrait for friends and relatives back home. It was easy to imagine the earnest young mother supervising the scrubbing and dressing, doing what she could to show how well things were going in their new home, how normal things were in this new place and how well they had preserved the order which they had brought West with them.

But relatives who received the picture might have easily gotten the wrong impression, for in spite of the careful costuming, the family's facial expressions sent a different message. The mouths turned down at the corners, the too-straight-on gazes suggested a certain weary resignation as if worn down with the struggling they had simply given in to acceptance, the easy treason that tempts those tired of trying to cope with a situation that is somehow more than they had bargained for.

"They have given up," Fuller said, looking up from the photograph."

"Maybe not," David suggested. "There could be a scientific explanation for it."

"Scientific?"

"The old collodion photographic plates were very slow. They required very long exposure times. Five to six seconds depending on the light. Long exposure times were no problem for landscape photography, but for portraits it was a different matter. It was nearly impossible for the subject to maintain a natural smile for six seconds, so . . . ."

"So, that accounts for the dour expressions."

"Exactly," said David.

Fuller studied the photograph again."You know, Walton, you're a veritable storehouse of information."

"Just pleased to be helpful," David replied with mock modesty. He took the book from Fuller and put it back on the floor."By the way, what did the newspaper have to say about the mistrial? Is it really true that it was granted because the judge said in his sentence that Hammit should hang because there were seven Democrats in Henson County and he ate five of them?" David laughed.

"I hadn't heard that one," Fuller said, "but according to the newspaper the mistrial was based on a legal point. In 1874, when the murders were committed this area around Henson was part of the Colorado Territory. By the time the trial took place, Henson was in the state of Colorado. Hammit couldn't be tried under Colorado state law because the murders were committed before Colorado was a state. Neither, contended Hammit's lawyer, could he be tried under Colorado Territorial law since that law was repealed when Colorado became a state."

"What a loophole!"

"Well, it saved him from hanging," Fuller said.

"But it wasn't enough to keep him out of prison. He was convicted again at the second trial in Gunther two years later," David pointed out. "What did our friends at the *Silver World* have to say about that?"

"I haven't gotten that far."

"We should check out the Gunther paper," David suggested.

"While we're there we can look at the transcript of the second trial."

"And we can ask your lawyer friend Brewster about the mistrial."

"Right."

"You know," said David, "when you think about it Hammit was tried twice for the same crime, wasn't he?"

"Some people have all the luck."

14 ✝✝✝✝

Two roads lead to Gunther from Henson. The direct route, now US Highway 49, follows the Lake Fork of the Gunther River due north for sixty miles. It is a paved all-weather road and the trip takes just over an hour. The other, known locally as the back way, climbs west from town to the top of the Cebolla Pass where, at timberline, it leaves the pavement and turning north winds down along the brushy headwaters of Los Alamos Creek, descending with the stream through forty miles of lonely ranchland to it's confluence with the main river two miles above Gunther.

The longer back way was more interesting for David and Fuller. This dirt road followed the track of the old Saguache-to-Silverdale toll road, the road Otto Meers was building when the bodies of Hammit's five companions were discovered and it was the same route Hammit had taken when he walked out from the gruesome campsite in the Henson Valley.

"It's still hard for me to believe Hammit walked out of here in the winter," David said as he steered over the rutted road.

"Forty miles," said Fuller. "Through the snow."

"And he must have had a pack," said David.

"And a load on his mind," Fuller quipped.

"Surely Hammit must have known he would eventually meet up with the other men in the party," said David. "The ones who stayed behind at Ouray's camp and that they would certainly ask about the others when they never showed up. You'd have thought he would have put together a better story."

"Than the one he told at the trial?"

"No. The story he told at the Agency."

"Oh, I don't know," said Fuller. "His story was fairly believable. Lost and starving, panicky with hunger and the cold, the others gang up on the weakest ones killing them one at a time and living off their bodies. Then only the two of them left, Bell tries to kill Hammit. Hammit kills Bell in self-defense. Hammit is not entirely blameless but was afraid of the others. Afraid for his own life. Under the circumstances he might get off as a victim. Especially since Bell tried to kill him too."

"Taking Miller's knife wasn't too smart," said David.

"Well," replied Fuller, "that seems natural enough. Why let a perfectly good knife go to waste?"

"What I don't understand," David said, puzzled, "is why he hung around the Agency for so long. It seems to me if he had really murdered those five men, he would have kept going. He could have disappeared."

"Maybe it happened like he said. Either version. Maybe he didn't kill them."

"But he did break out of jail," protested David.

"By then he could see the handwriting on the wall. The bodies had been discovered and he was scared. Finding the bodies all together made it pretty clear the men hadn't died one at a time like he said in his statement to Adams."

"Do you think he ate the bodies?" David asked.

"I'd be surprised if he didn't," said Fuller. "As you said, he had to have eaten something during all that time and even Hammit said there wasn't any game."

"I'll bet when survival was at stake cannibalism was more common than we think."

"Oh, I agree," said Fuller,"but no one wants to talk about it. It's pretty clear isn't it, that there was cannibalism on Hawthorne's expedition?"

"He denied it."

"What else could he do? It would have been such an indictment of his leadership. But that reference in his diary to 'events here in the mountains too awful to contemplate . . . . ' "

"And his comment about his guide that no one would walk ahead of him in starving times.

"'The custom of the sea,'" Fuller quoted. "That's how cannibalism was known in the British Admiralty. The 'defense of necessity.'"

"There is a certain gruesome logic to it though, isn't there? Using a dead man's body to ensure the survival of the living."

"Well, there is another practical matter," Fuller said. "Cannibalism leads to murder, doesn't it? That's why the taboo. I mean, let's say one of the members of a starving party dies and the others eat his body to stay alive. That's arguable from a theologic point of view. But what next? What if no one dies and the others are still starving? Where does it stop? Once you've crossed that line, there's no turning back. The fabric of the group begins to unravel. The survivors become prey. No one can let his guard down for a minute. Or sleep for that matter."

"The newspapers certainly did their best to play on the cannibalism. But even if Hammit did eat the bodies, that doesn't mean he murdered the men."

"No, but it's awfully suspicious, isn't it?"

*   *   *

At Los Pinos, the site of the old Ute Indian Agency, David pulled the car over and stopped. He set the hand brake and crossed his arms on top of the steering wheel. Surrounded by the Cochetopa Hills, the empty valley widened out into a broad level grassland two miles across, and on the flat of the meadow the stream, which had been in such a hurry to leave the timberline, meandered through the meadow in wide slow curves catching its breath before resuming its noisy dash to the river. Above the aspen and sagebrush hills in all directions the peaks of the San Juan cordillera pressed up against the low gray sky. In the pastoral security of this mountain valley the Tabeguache Utes—the Blue Sky People, the People of the Shining Mountains—had made their last stand. Not against the armed blue firepower of cavalry troops, but against the alien faceless torque of federal bureaucracy.

The Utes were nomads and before the whites came west they followed the migrating herds of elk and buffalo over a range of 150,000 square miles from the plains east of Denver to the slickrock canyons of southern Utah. They were shy and private but fiercely territorial and other tribes respected their fearsome reputation for defending their ancestral range. Even the first westering immigrants avoided the Ute homeland. But in time the pressure of white settlement increased, and with each successive wave of immigrants the People of The Shining Mountains were pushed deeper into the high ground of their mountain stronghold. Finally, crowded from their freedom by a series of broken treaties the Utes retreated to this last remnant of their wild refuge. Ironically, it was the good luck of an Indian that cost the Utes their home.

In the spring of 1850, a group of prospectors—Cherokee Indians and their white relatives—left the played-out goldfields of Dahlonega, Georgia and headed for the promise of California. At the eastern foothills of the Rockies near the site that would be selected for Denver, they stopped to pan the promising gravel bars of Cherry Creek and found the first flakes of Colorado gold. The yield was small and they moved on. But those who heard their story remembered and eight years later their lusty "Eureka's" echoed out of the hills and across the plains.

Desperate men raced west determined to reach Pike's Peak or bust. Finding the best ground already claimed they pushed farther into the mountains, into South Park and the Arkansas Valley, and up the quiet canyons, tearing at the earth and leaving ugly ochre sores. The Ute fortress was under siege.

Spanish-Americans, freed by the Treaty of Guadalupe-Hidalgo of 1848, moved north from the upper Rio Grande into the fertile Antonio Valley, settling the land and scattering the herds. Ute leaders were hastily called to Abiquiu where they signed the first treaty between the Ute nation and the new government in the West, acknowledging the authority of the United States in return for a territorial allotment in western Colorado. Their eastern range was gone.

Still the settlers came. By 1868, blown west by the storm of war, tens of thousands of veterans had drifted into the Rockies seeking land and gold. The cultural confrontations increased and in 1873, the Brunot Treaty ceded the San Juan Mountains to the greedy boomers.

The remaining Utes, bewildered and melancholy, were ordered to the Los Pinos Agency where, in this remote mountain valley near the center of their universe, they collected like the residual waters of a once great lake. There, for seven years, while the newspapers in Denver called for an end to the "Ute Menace", these trusting few lived on government provisions, captives in their own land, dependant on the meager welfare of the Agency and the bureaus which had betrayed them. One warm day, in the spring of 1880, the two hundred who remained of four thousand were herded together, prisoners of a civil war, and marched under heavy guard to their new reservation in the flats of northern Utah, too far from home to see their shining mountains.

David still sat leaning on the steering wheel, looking out over the empty landscape. The old Agency building was gone, its roof pulled down, its adobe walls eroded flat. Rounded clumps of sage replaced the triangular geometry of the teepee villages. Smoky twisted clouds, moved with the wind over the valley darkening the ground except where it was lit by sheet-like patches of sunlight that danced over the grass like bright spirits.

"Are you slipping back in time?" Fuller asked with a smile.

David hadn't realized he had been daydreaming. He turned to face Fuller who had been watching him across the car seat.

"I guess I was," David admitted. "I tend to do that"

"I think you feel a little cheated you didn't live then."

"You know, sometimes I think I do. How about you?"

"Not really. I'm too spoiled by creature comforts. I like following my heros at a safer distance."

"But it is a seductive thought, isn't it, to think we could go back to the way things were then. We've never really gotten over our love affair with the frontier. It was never consummated. It all happened too fast. Fifty years maybe, to get to know half a continent? We passed through that period before we had time to come to terms with it. We never got closure. We are like children who weren't allowed to go to their father's funeral. It's a form of maturation arrest. We still dream maybe things can be like they once were and seeing this country is all it takes to start the dreaming. Imagine seeing all this for the first time before the power lines and the paved roads, before we got at it with progress when it was so much less spoiled by the things we do to the places we love. Maybe I'm just a sentimental hold-out but can't we be spared a little romance? What's wrong with a little wonder anyway?

"You know, it's not fashionable now to be nostalgic about the West."

"That's what I've heard."

*　　　*　　　*

In Gunther there was more traffic than usual for an August afternoon. Red, white and blue bunting hung from wires stretched over the wide main street, block after block with kaleidoscopic repetition, and on every corner wind-bulged banners announced SKY HI DAYS to cars passing through the colorful tunnel.

"The Fair," Fuller said. "I forgot about that. We'll never get a room." David and Fuller had planned to spend the afternoon reviewing the transcript of Hammit's second trial and then stay overnight to meet with Fuller's lawyer friend the following day.

"It doesn't start till tomorrow," David pointed out, "but from the looks of this crowd we'd better try to get a place to stay before we go to the courthouse."

There was no vacancy at the Parkview Motel, David's preference, or at the Elkhorn or the River Bend. The Tomichi Inn had one room, a family suite. That would have to do. By the time they got back to town it was one fifteen. Anxious to get started on the transcript, they skipped lunch and went directly to the courthouse.

"I hate to disappoint you gentlemen," the clerk said with practiced gravity, "but we have no records of the Hammit trial."

David looked at Fuller. Here we go again, David thought. A quick glance told him Fuller was thinking the same thing.

"You mean the records are gone?" Fuller said, with annoyed disbelief.

"There never were any records," the clerk said matter-of-factly. "None were ever prepared."

"But there must be some mistake, "Fuller began. "In Henson . . . ."

The clerk, his eyes closed, one palm raised, interrupted him. "I know, I know," he said, an impatient edge in his voice. "Hammit was tried in Henson and a mistrial was declared and he was retried here," he recited. "But believe me, there is no record of the trial here. People have been coming here for years wanting to see the records of the second trial. I tell them all the same thing." He bit off each word. "It is simply not available."

Fuller looked at the floor composing himself. "Would it be possible to see the District Attorney?" he said in a measured tone.

"Of course," replied the clerk, still sitting, "His office is right down there." He pointed down the hall.

He was in but busy, so David and Fuller waited. After an hour, they were shown in. The young attorney was sympathetic but could do no more than confirm what the clerk had already told them.

"But isn't it customary to keep a record of trial proceedings," Fuller asked.

"Of course it is now," the attorney said, "but apparently at that time a record was prepared only if there was an appeal. Everything was copied by hand, you see."

"And there was no appeal?"

"Apparently not."

"Well," Fuller said, turning to David, "does this have a familiar ring to it?"

"It does, doesn't it? Deja vu."

"Beg your pardon?" the attorney said.

"Oh," said Fuller, "the same thing happened to us when we were researching another project a year or so ago. All the records we needed seemed to have disappeared."

"I'm sorry to have to be the one to give you the bad news. I think your best bet might be the newspaper accounts."

"We had hoped for something a little more objective," Fuller said.

Fuller sat for a moment considering what the attorney had said then turned to see if David had any questions.

94

David shook his head.

"Well," Fuller said, putting his hands on his knees signalling he was ready to leave, "Thank you for your time."

"I'm sorry I couldn't be of any help. If there is anything else . . . ."

"Actually," Fuller said, as he stood, "there is one thing. Are the court recorder's notes available?"

"Not that I know of. Probably they were destroyed."

*   *   *

"Come right this way," the editor said as David and Fuller followed him down the hall. "We keep back issues in here. It's our archives room. Rather dingy, I'm afraid, but right now it's the only place we have for them." He showed them into a small room.

Bundles of newspapers were stacked on metal shelves lining the four walls and extending from floor to ceiling. "Everything before 1900 is in here," the editor explained. "As far as I know, every single issue," he said proudly. "Please feel free to stay as long as you like. We don't close the building till ten. The papers you're interested in are right here." He walked to the shelf and patted a stack of newspapers. "They are indexed by year. Please try to put them back in the same order. Helps us find them."

"Of course," Fuller said.

"Now," the editor said, "if there is anything you need, just let me know

"Thank you," said Fuller. "You have been very kind."

The editor smiled and left, closing the door behind him. Fuller then turned to David.

"Well," said Fuller, "how do you want to do this?"

"The second trial began in August of 1886. Let's just take down this whole stack," he said straining to lift the bundle of papers, "and divide them up." He put the bundle on the table. "You check one while I check another. There won't be many. The trial only lasted a few days as I recall."

Each took a paper and began to read silently. After a minute Fuller spoke.

"This sort of sets the tone," Fuller said. "Listen. This is on page one, right next to the background story on Hammit. 'A Mississippi Negress killed two four-year-old children and made a stew of some of the flesh, pickling the remainder. The discovery of the bodies led to her confession, whereupon her neighbors burned her alive.' "

David rolled his eyes at the ceiling and resumed reading. In a few minutes Fuller broke the silence. "Get a load of this. It appeared after the first day of the trial. Again front page. Right under the account of the trial proceedings. 'Morris Connecticut: George Lockwood, the ravisher and murderer was taken from his cell last night and hanged to a tree near the scene of the crime.' "

They looked at each other and shook their heads. "It's amazing the paper could get away with that," David said.

"The honorable profession," Fuller replied sarcastically.

The two men worked through the afternoon, reading seven papers, making notes and occasionally pointing out something. By 4:30 they were finished.

"Well," David said. He leaned back in his chair, stretched his arms over his head and propped his feet on the table "What do you think?"

"I think the *Gunther Press-Review* and the *Silver World* were a lot alike," said Fuller.

"You don't suppose they had the same owner? " David suggested.

"Now that would be interesting, wouldn't it?" Fuller said. He folded the newspaper he had been reading and scanned the front page for a second time. "The crowd filed out of the room," he quoted in his broadcast voice, "and thirteen years after his heinous crime Alfred Hammit, the cannibal, the monster, is disposed of." He looked up at David. "Cannibal? Monster?"

"Sounds like the Henson trial all over again."

"It's not surprising Hammit was found guilty again is it?"

"Not really," David said. "But he didn't help himself any. Did you see the descriptions of how he behaved at the trial?"

"You mean like telling the prosecuting attorney to shut up!"

"You suppose that's really true?"

"Who knows, but they never seemed to miss a chance to portray him as some kind of maniac." Fuller quoted again. "Hammit detailed his adventures in a wild and incoherent manner, waving his mutilated hand in the air and haranguing the jury in broken sentences."

"There's your monster," said David.

"At the first trial Hammit was convicted of killing Bell, right?"

"Right."

"But at the retrial he was convicted of killing all five men. How can that be?"

"I know," David agreed. "That struck me too."

"We'll have to ask Brewster about that tomorrow." Fuller made a note on a pad in front of him.

"And did you notice, the prosecution kept harping away about that Wells Fargo bank note of Miller's that Hammit was supposed to have had."

"And Meers, the only witness to that and he never showed up to be cross-examined. How can a witness just not show up? That's something else I want to ask Brewster about."

"And what do you think Hammit meant in his final statement? Let's see, how did he put it? Here. 'I have been sentenced unjustly. In later years this will be cleared up, for there has never been a case where a man was unjustly sentenced that sooner or later it was not cleared up. There is this Mr. Downs, he is an old man, but if he don't die a sudden death, he can state this whole mystery to the public. On his death bed he will straighten all this up.' "

"Who is Downs?" David turned to Fuller.

"Sounds like he might be the key to this case, doesn't it?"

15 ✝✝✝✝

It was light when David awoke. At first the white ceiling confused him, then he remembered they had come to Gunther to see Brewster. He rubbed the sleep from his face and sat up in the bed, supporting himself on his elbows. Across the room beyond the end of the bed the window framed the sky and the morning mountains and Fuller who was sitting on the balcony reading. David got up and joined him. The soft air was cool and under the spruce trees around the motel the ground was streaked with their long shadows.

"Did you stay out here all night?"

"Had to." Fuller joked without looking up. "To get away from your snoring. You up for the whole day?"

"I haven't decided yet." Despite wanting to, David found it difficult to get up early. He walked to the edge of the balcony extended his arms, stretched and leaned forward on the metal railing. "Pretty nice out here, isn't it?" he said, inhaling, deeply. "Where'd you get that coffee?"

"In the kitchen of our suite," Fuller replied with an aristocratic tone.

"Oh, that's right," David remembered. He turned to go to the kitchen.

"Bring me a refill, would you?" Fuller asked. Without looking up from reading he handed his cup back over his shoulder .

"Certainly Sir," David replied in his best butler voice. "Shall I draw your bath?"

"Just coffee, Jenkins," said Fuller, picking up on the vignette. It was a game the two enjoyed. They shared the easy testy camaraderie that develops among boys and is nurtured by men friends.

David returned with the cups. He handed one to Fuller and, balancing the other carefully, sat down beside him in the metal motel chair and propped his bare feet on the railing. The mountains were close and unavoidable. The denim sky was stretched tight over the morning. Rounded sage hills the color of elk crowded together along the river and shaded the creases where their smooth flanks met.

"Are you working?" David said over his cup.

Fuller looked up from the pad of notes, stretched lazily and leaned back against the chair, hands clasped over his head. "Why would Hammit lie about his age?" he said.

"Who is Hammit?" David said playfully.

Fuller smiled. "Aren't we feeling frisky this morning?" Fuller took the pad from his lap and put it down beside his chair.

"When did he lie about his age?" David asked.

"At the second trial," Fuller replied. "In the newspaper account of the sentencing, Hammit was quoted as saying that he was thirty-four. Before the first trial, The *Silver World* quoted him as saying he was born in 1842. That would make him forty-two."

"Maybe he didn't even know?" David suggested.

"Maybe," Fuller wondered, "but if he lied about something as insignificant as that . . . ?"

"He did seem to change his stories a lot, didn't he," David agreed.

"He lied about his age. He lied to Adams at the time of the first confession at Los Pinos. And those are just the lies we know about. Did he lie about having the Wells Fargo note? Did he lie when he told the back-tracking party he was lost? Did he lie about shooting Bell in the abdomen? Or in the head?" Fuller leaned forward, elbows on his knees. "You know, I think I'm getting down on Hammit. I'm suspicious. I'm beginning to think he killed them all. He seems to have lied about things that didn't matter."

"Well, if he did kill them all, he was really foolish to hang around the Agency so long. He could have easily disappeared."

"He probably thought the bodies would never be found," Fuller said cynically. "He thought they would rot there in the wilderness. He never dreamed that within six months the bodies would be in the middle of a boom town."

Fuller picked up his note pad and thumbed the pages slowly. David sat thinking.

"Have you thought about where you want to be buried?" David said.

Fuller slowly looked up at David, purposely dramatizing the gesture. "Did you say buried?"

"Umm," David nodded.

"Well," Fuller said with a soft laugh, "I've got to admit I haven't given it much thought. What brought that up?"

"Looking at the mountains reminded me."

"The mountains?"

"Every year when we came to the mountains on vacation my father would stop the car on top of the Continental Divide, at Spring Creek Pass, so my brother and I could pee in the spring there."

Fuller, amused, shook his head slowly in disbelief.

"It was a family tradition," David shrugged. "Funny how things like that get started."

Fuller's expression suggested he was equally baffled.

"But my father always pointed out that it was a symbolic act since half of the pee would eventually go to the Pacific Ocean and half to the Atlantic."

"Quite an object lesson," said Fuller, still not sure if David was serious. "It's too much to ask I suppose, what peeing in a spring has to do with being buried?"

"Well," David went on, "I got to thinking. Kids move around a lot these days and no matter where you are buried, it's bound to be inconvenient for them if they ever want to visit your grave. So I decided that when I die, I want to be cremated and have my ashes scattered on the Continental Divide. In time, at least theoretically, part of the ashes will wash down the Rio Grande watershed to the Atlantic and part will wash down into the Gunther River through Colorado to the Pacific. That way, Ol' Dad won't be anywhere. He'll be everywhere. No traveling." He sat back, pleased with himself. "Like it?"

Fuller, chin in his hand was looking at David.

"Well,? What do you think?"

"Corny," Fuller said flatly.

"I thought that's what you would say," said David. "You know Fuller, your trouble is you have no romance in your soul."

"Well," Fuller said, shifting in his chair to exaggerate the change of subject, "how about some breakfast before we see Brewster? You have been up," he looked at his watch, "for almost fifteen minutes now. You must have thought about breakfast?"

"As a matter of fact," David said, feigning resentment, "I was thinking about breakfast. How about a couple'a dozen Early Bird donuts? Nature's perfect food."

"You eat like you have a death-wish."

"Flour and animal fat and sugar. What could be more natural than that?"

"Let me think," Fuller pretended.

David stood up. "Well, Sir-King, shall we go together, or do you want me to bring them out here to you?"

David slowed behind the line of traffic turning into the fair grounds. Already the parking lot was nearly filled with rows of cars and pick-ups and stock trailers. Along the midway, tawdry in its daytime clothes, crowds milled among the concession stands and stood in lines waiting their turn on the spinning rides. Floating above it all the hurdy-gurdy-organ-and-oom-pah music rose and fell smoothly in time with the turnings of the merry-go-round.

At the other end of the fairgrounds, near the painted white fence of the rodeo arena a quieter crowd had gathered. Young men with numbers on their backs, some with straw hats, some with long hair and gimmie caps, looking more like truck drivers than cowboys, carried saddles, fussed with hay bales and blankets, stood talking in small groups or hunkered down in the shade alone waiting for a ride that might make them a little money or make them limp for life while their horses, tied to stock trailers and fence rails, dozed in the sun.

"Did you ever do any rodeoing?" David knew Fuller had been raised on a ranch.

"My brother and I did some roping. Heading-and-heeling. None of the rough-stock stuff."

"Were you any good?"

"We thought we were. In the summers we rodeoed on the weekends and during the week we hired out to local ranchers, helping them vaccinate their stock. At one time we figured we must have roped ten thousand steers."

"You must have been pretty good!"

"Anybody who does something ten thousand times is bound to get good at it."

"Ever get hurt?"

"Nearly. When I was first learning. I almost lost my thumb."

"Get stepped on?"

"Rope burn," Fuller clarified. "Some of the steers we were roping weighed two thousand pounds. One took off on me before I got the rope dallied tight. I wasn't holding the rope right and it burned right through my glove. Nearly burned my thumb off."

"How are you supposed to hold it?" David asked.

Fuller turned to David and held out his hand to demonstrate.

"When you throw the loop, you end up with the rope coming out between your first finger and your thumb, with your fingers curled underneath. Like this. If the steer runs to the right, away from the horse, the rope can cut right across your thumb. The right way to hold it is like this." Fuller turned his hand over and grasped the imaginary rope, fingers on top, thumb extended back toward his body. "This way, if he runs on you, the rope comes out off the fat of your hand, and it won't cut."

"Ever win any money?"

"About half of what it took to pay my entry fees."

The car ahead of David turned in at the fairground gate. As David drove past, he acknowledged the gate attendant. It was a small gesture, fingers of the right hand merely lifted together from the steering wheel. A small wave, but unmistakable and one still seen if you know when to look, when oncoming cars pass on western highways. The gate attendant noticed and responded to it with a smile and a quick lift of his chin.

Fuller laughed softly to himself. "I haven't thought about that in years. My brother and I thought we were really going to hit the big time. All in all, we figured we drank up more than we won. Couldn't stay out of the road houses. Honky-tonks. Didn't he love to dance."

"Your brother?"

"He was crazy for it. He could dance for hours. And some of the places we went." He shook his head, remembering. "Some of them had chicken wire fencing around the stage so the musicians wouldn't get hit with flying beer bottles."

"It's a wonder you didn't get beat to a pulp."

"We probably would have if we hadn't played it right, but we had it figured out. Or rather he did. My brother."

"And . . .?"

"He said, always dance with the ugly women. They always appreciate it and you never get in trouble."

*   *   *

"Come on in!" Brewster bellowed, walking from behind the cluttered desk to shake the men's hands. "The last time I saw you two, you were about to take on the whole Hawthorne family. "

Brewster was an old friend of Fuller's. He had helped Fuller with some personal matters when he was dismissed from the college and David and Fuller had sought his advice the year before when they were working on the Hawthorne book. Brewster was older than Fuller, perhaps sixty-five or so, tall, overweight and slightly senatorial. He had an open easy manner, a tendency to be theatrical and wavy gray hair badly in need of combing. He wore a plaid western shirt and a loose bolo tie with a silver and turquoise thunderbird pull. He looked like a three-term politician on vacation.

"You're looking good," Fuller said as Brewster pumped his hand. How've you been?"

"Hell Fuller, if I felt any better they'd have to put a guard on me."

"I see you've straightened things up in here," Fuller said gesturing around the room. "This looks like a graduate student's room."

"Oh, don't let that put you off," Brewster laughed. "I know exactly where everything is. Sit down. Sit down," he waved them to a seat. Brewster sat behind his desk and put his black five-stitch boots up on the corner. "Well now," he said, folding his hands across his full shirt front, "what are you two up to now? It must be trouble or you wouldn't be here."

"We're onto another murder case," Fuller said

"Haw!" Brewster laughed. "If you keep this up, the FBI is going to have to put you two on the payroll. Tell me about it. Who is the murderer this time?"

"Alfred Hammit," Fuller stated.

Brewster dropped his feet to the floor and leaned forward on the desk, eyes narrowed with disapproval. "Fascinating case. The worst miscarriage of justice the state's legal system has ever known. What can I do to help?"

"Tell us about it," Fuller said.

"Where do you want me to begin?"

"You pick," said Fuller.

"Well," Brewster paused, organizing his thoughts, "as far as the trials were concerned there's no way Hammit could have gotten a fair trial in Henson or Gunther, either one. The defense should have insisted on a change of venue. Everyone in both towns had already decided Hammit was guilty."

"We have been reading through the old newspapers," Fuller said.

"Then you know what I mean," Brewster said.

"Why didn't Hammit's lawyer ask for a change of venue?" Fuller asked.

"He did!" Brewster replied, indignant. "At both trials. The judge denied it both times. But that was only one issue. At the first trial . . . " He paused. "Have you read the transcript?"

"I have," said David.

"Well, then," Brewster continued, "you may have noticed that the judge in his charge to the jury suggested that, in arriving at their verdict, they should consider the apparent contradictions in Hammit's testimony, and his possession of property of the deceased unless these things had been satisfactorily explained by the evidence presented. In doing so, of course, he placed the burden of proof on Hammit, that is, to prove that he was not guilty. His attorney objected, of course, and the judge later rephrased his instructions but it was too much to ask the jurors to sort out the meaning of the conflicting instructions."

"So the judge may have biased the jurors right from the start?" said Fuller.

"Precisely," Brewster said.

"What about the appeal of the first trial?" Fuller said. "What was actually the basis of the appeal?"

"It was based on an important legal point." Brewster was becoming more animated. "In 1874, when the alleged murders occurred Henson was in Colorado Territory. After statehood, by an act of the Colorado Legislature the murder section of the general law was repealed and replaced by a new law, but unfortunately without any savings clause. This act took effect in 1881, after the alleged murder and before Hammit's trial. Hammit's lawyer argued, therefore, that Hammit could not be tried under the old law, since it had been repealed at the time of the trial nor could he be tried under the new state law which had not been passed until after the alleged crime had been committed."

"What is a savings clause?" Fuller asked.

"Essentially," Brewster explained, "a savings clause would have preserved the state's right to prosecute, under the new state law, murders committed before the repeal of the old territorial law. Omitting the clause at the time of the repeal was a legislative blunder."

"So that's why Hammit got a new trial" Fuller said.

"That's right," said Brewster. "The appeal went to the Colorado Supreme Court and he was granted a new trial.

"Why," said David, "was Hammit tried for the murder of one man at the first trial and at the second trial, the murder of all five?"

"Ah," said Brewster, "it's worse than that. At the second trial, the judge ordered that all five indictments would be consolidated! Never in the history of criminal jurisprudence has there been a precedent for trying anyone for five different indictments of murder before one jury. You see, the missing proof on one charge is supplied by implication from the others. For instance, if all the murdered men were said to have died of hatchet blows, but this could not be proven in the case of one of the victims, the cause of his death would be implied by the cause of death of the others. But," he went on," that would be speculation and speculation is contrary to the sworn obligation of the jurors."

"Surely the defense objected to that?" said Fuller.

"No," said Brewster, "and there is no reasonable explanation for that."

"Actually," said Fuller, "now that you mention it the prosecution could not have proved the death of all the men was caused by hatchet blows. When the bodies of the men were found, one man's skull was missing."

"Right," said Brewster, "and it never turned up. And," he emphasized, "did you notice that the coroner was never called to testify in either trial?"

"No, I didn't" said Fuller, "but we did notice that at the second trial Meers never showed up."

"But," said Brewster, raising his finger to make the point, "his testimony, which was considered so crucial and so damning at the first trial, was related to the jury by the prosecution, a clear violation of legal procedure. The defense should have insisted that Meers appear for cross examination. Either that or that any reference to his testimony be deleted."

"Another blunder for the defense," said Fuller.

"Why wasn't Meers summoned?" David asked.

"He was," said Brewster. "Meers was to be the last witness for the state. He just didn't show up."

"How could that be?" said David.

Brewster smiled, knowingly. "I won't say that some men are above the law, but . . ." He paused to select the right word. "Some men think they are."

"But the defense should have insisted," said Fuller.

"Of course he should have," replied Brewster shrugging, "but there you are."

"Poor old Hammit didn't stand a chance," David said.

"I'm not saying Hammit was innocent, mind you," Brewster said. "Only that the whole legal proceeding was shall we say, to be kind, sub-optimal."

"Who was Downs?" asked Fuller.

"James Downs," Brewster smiled. His chair squeaked as he leaned back against it. "He was Justice of the Peace in Saguache when Hammit was arrested."

"Why would Hammit have said that Downs could have cleared up the whole thing?"

"Well" said Brewster, "that's an interesting point. Some years after the trial an attorney in Denver named Soderholm got interested in the case and worked for a while to get Hammit paroled. He went all over the state interviewing people who knew Hammit or anything about the situation. Downs was one of the men Soderholm interviewed. He had been with McNutt and the men who took Hammit back to look for the bodies. McNutt, you will recall, testified that when they got close to where the bodies were eventually found that Hammit said he was lost."

"I remember reading that," David said.

"Sounds suspicious, doesn't it?" Fuller added.

"Well," Brewster went on, "Downs had a different story. He told Soderholm that when they back-tracked with Hammit to try to find the bodies, Hammit led them straight up the mountain to a large park just on the east side of the divide. There Hammit said the place looked familiar and that if they went over the mountain he might be able to locate the campsite."

"Why didn't they?" David asked.

"Downs told Soderholm that McNutt was in charge of the party and that he was convinced that Hammit was lying. So they all turned back."

"So Downs might have actually supported Hammit's story?" suggested David.

"Right," said Brewster.

"Why wasn't Downs called to testify?" Fuller said.

Brewster shrugged.

"Tell me about the appeal of the second trial?" David said.

"Ah, yes," Brewster replied. "That's another story. Immediately after the trial in Gunther Hammit's attorney wanted to file an appeal, but apparently Hammit didn't have the money so he was sent to prison in Canyon City. He was destitute. After three years Soderholm, as a result of his interviews, became convinced that Hammit was innocent and helped him raise the money for an appeal."

"Hammit's new attorney filed the appeal seeking Hammit's release from prison in which he argued, as I mentioned, that it had not been proper to consolidate the five indictments. The appeal was filed in 1889, at the time of the expiration of the first sentence for manslaughter, considering time for good behavior."

"And . . .?"

"The appeal was denied."

"But why, exactly?" David asked.

"Here's the zinger," Brewster said. "In their response to the petition the

Supreme Court ruled that if Hammit did not agree with the conduct of the trial he should have appealed the verdict immediately afterwards, since any errors committed during the trial were reviewed only by appeal. However, since there had been no appeal at the time of the second trial, no written record was prepared. In the absence of the record there could be no appeal."

"Incredible," Fuller said.

"At the time," Brewster went on, "the decision was widely criticized by the legal community. Many agreed there were substantial grounds for an appeal and accused the court of taking refuge in legalistic procedure. But after a while the furor quieted down and nothing more came of it."

"What a scandal," Fuller said, disgusted.

"Shameful," said Brewster. "Like I said, the worst miscarriage of justice the state has known." The three men were quiet for a moment. "You know, you two should go to Denver to see Soderholm's papers," Brewster said again. "Maybe they will help some." Brewster leaned back in his chair and locked his fingers behind his head. "Confounding case, isn't it? Probably never will be settled."

"Then we'll just have to dig up the bodies," said David. Fuller looked at David, surprised. They hadn't talked about that.

Brewster studied David over his glasses, trying to decide if David was serious. "You can do that," Brewster said solemnly. "You're serious?"

"Yes," said Fuller, without checking with David. "We just don't know how to go about it."

Brewster nodded slowly. "Well," he said, thinking, "as far as legal matters go, you'll need to publish a notice of exhumation. I can help you with that. And you will need the written permission of the land owner."

"That will be no problem," David said. "Dub owns the land," he reminded Fuller.

"A friend of ours," Fuller explained to Brewster.

"You will want some archaeological advice," Brewster said.

"Definitely" said Fuller. "Do you have anyone in mind?"

"Well, Brewster said, "as a matter-of-fact, there is an old friend of mine in Santa Fe who might be willing to help. Ernest Cowan. He's a professor of anthropology at St. Michael's College there. He also has a position with the Indian Arts Research Center. His main interest is forensic anthropology. He does a lot of consulting work for law enforcement agencies. Actually, he helped identify the body of Josef Mengele down in Argentina."

"Sounds like just the person we need to talk to," David said.

Brewster reached deliberately across the desk and flipped up the top of a metal address book. "I can help you with that too." He read off a number to himself, moving his lips, then snapped the log shut and dialed the phone. Brewster leaned back in his chair looking very businesslike, now more than a little interested and obviously pleased with himself that he was in a position to help.

"Professor Cowan's office, please." The three men waited. "Yes," Brewster said into the phone, "this is Ed Brewster. I'm calling Professor Cowan. Is he in?" Pause. "Of course." Brewster winked at David. "We're in luck." Brewster was smiling. "Ernie!" he said. "Ed Brewster. How are you? I know. Fine, fine." Brewster laughed. "Listen Ernie, a couple of friends of mine need your help. They are doing some research on an old murder case and they're getting to the point now that they really need to exhume the bodies. Real old. The Alfred Hammit case. 1874. Yes. Yes. No, I don't think that will be a problem. A friend of theirs owns the land. Yes. I can help them with that part. Right. Tell you what I'll do. I'll have them send you their CVs and a letter outlining their proposal. Right. Jack Fuller and David Walton. Right. You should hear from them soon. I will. Say, isn't it about time you came up here for some decent fishing?" Brewster laughed. "Good, Ernie. Call me. Tell Mattie 'Hello'. I will. Thanks, Ernie. You bet."

Brewster leaned forward and hung up the receiver. "Well." He folded his hands in front of him on the desk and looked back and forth from David to Fuller. "It's all set."

"Great," said David.

"Here's the address," Brewster said, writing, "and the phone number in case you need to call him. He's a nice guy. You will like him." Brewster held out the paper to David who took it, looked at it briefly then folded it and tucked it into his shirt pocket.

"That's a big help, Ed," Fuller said.

"My pleasure," Brewster said. "Be sure to tell me how all this all comes out. I have an old lawyer's interest in this case."

"What should we do now?" Fuller said.

"Well," Brewster answered, "check with your friend and make sure he doesn't mind your digging up the bodies. Get a written statement from him, okay? Then I'll arrange to publish the notice of exhumation." He was making hasty notes on a yellow legal pad as he talked. "Probably the *Denver Post*. We have thirty days after that." He paused to look at a calendar on his desk. "From a legal point of view, assuming no relatives object, you should be ready to go by, let's say, September first?" He looked up at the two men.

David shifted restlessly in his chair.

"Give me the murdered men's names again," Brewster said.

Fuller spelled out the names of the five men while Brewster wrote.

"There," Brewster said, looking over the pad, "that should do it. I'll let you know if I hear from any of the relatives."

"You've been a big help, Ed," Fuller said. "As usual."

"My pleasure."

*   *   *

Professor Cowan answered Fuller's letter within a week. He was interested in the project and thought he might be able to help, suggesting they call his office and arrange for an appointment. Fuller called that same day.

16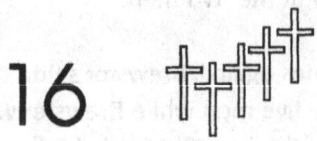

Highway 149 is the only paved road through the San Juan Mountains. On the map it stands out clearly against the empty space, a thin black line winding it's way southeast more like a river than a road, it's continuity broken only once, midway along it's tortuous course by a small black circle that marks the site of Henson, Colorado. Beyond Henson's tiny icon, the resolute little line wiggles it's way through the x-x-x 's of the Continental Divide, finds the thin blue headwaters of the Rio Grande and at The Forks, yields its black identity to the red of U.S. 10 bending south along the river into New Mexico.

For migrating Ute families this pass was the traditional trail from their mountain hunting grounds to their winter camps in the pinon and mesa country south of the Sierra Platta. For sandaled and gray-robed columns of Spanish friars it cut two days off the trek from the missions of California to the pueblos of northern New Spain. And for solitary trappers with fur bundles and visions of fandangos, it was a shortcut from the beaver-rich waters of the White River Basin to the dancing and trading in Taos.

In favorable weather a man on foot could make the 250-mile trip from Henson to Santa Fe in ten days. On a good horse with no pack animals and a little luck, maybe five. In a green Volvo wagon two men could leave Henson after breakfast, stop for coffee and a sweet roll in Del Norte, and still be in Santa Fe for lunch.

David steered to the left taking the fork that crossed the river at the south end of the valley just beyond Dub's ranch. As they swung around to the east and began the climb to the top of Cannibal Plateau they passed the six white posts of the fenced enclosure that marked the Hammit massacre site. David's eyes were drawn to it as they had been every time he passed it since that summer when his father had first told him the Hammit story. Fuller saw him looking.

"Won't be long now," Fuller said.

"Here's to Professor Cowan," David responded, toasting with his coffee cup.

At the top of the pass they stopped as they always did to look down on the valley and out at the broken blue-gray cordillera of the Uncompahgre range. For the moment satisfied, they drove on descending along the eastern slope through spruce and fir forests crowded close along the road then lower down in ecological order through umber stands of Ponderosa pines, through bright and shadowed aspen groves, through a broadening series of U-shaped, gray-saged valleys to the river.

At Alamosa they turned south into the valley of the upper Rio Grande and for two hours followed the broad corridor walled in between the Sangre de Cristos and the San Juan Mountains toward a point on the horizon where their blue parallels seemed to meet. The road kept to the contoured foothills west of the river, zig-zagging to stay on the high ground. To the east across the khaki valley the abrupt and serrate fault line of the Sangre de Cristos, backlit by the morning sun, stood propped against the edge of the earth like a faded band saw cut-out. The hard light was so clear, the simple seamless sky so pure, the widened space so vast that judging distance was impossible and David felt cleansed by the feelings that washed over him.

He remembered then that occasionally while living in New Hampshire, he had glanced absentmindedly up from some outdoor business to see what appeared to be a distant denim range piled halfway up the sky. He was never prepared for those moments and for a pleasant instant he would get a familiar satisfying rush and a desire to drive to them, drive up into them as far as the car would go and walk among their canyons and secret places. On those days he would realize again how much he missed the West and how important it was for him to someday live where he could always see these wilder mountains.

He stopped the car long enough to break off a branch of sagebrush and put it on the dashboard in the sun. Immediately the familiar, piquant perfume filled the car. Fuller smiled.

As they drove on to the south the sun rose higher in the sky and in the brassy light the landscape took on a shadowed bold relief. Dark canyons cut the mountainsides and strut-like ridges, their south slopes bright and nearly bare, buttressed the tilted slopes. The temperature rose with the mounting sun and dried the land as they approached. The cool colors of the mountains slowly yielded to the earthen tones of the high desert. Over the warming valley floor scalloped white cumulus clouds bloomed atop their invisible thermal pedestals like huge flat bottomed peonies.

By the time they reached Antonito the transition to northern New Mexico was almost complete. Widely spaced juniper and pinons had replaced the pines. Networks of dry streambeds and arroyos with eroded fluted walls etched the sandy land, leaving it as tanned and finely worked as a piece of hand-tooled leather. Die-cut mesas, their cliffs being reduced to talus, squared off the skyline. Along the road log cabins gave way to low territorial style houses with pleated red tin roofs and painted white window frames a foot above the ground and rain-washed adobe walls dried and wrinkled and sunbrowned the color of gingersnaps. And out across the grassy plain as if arrested in their march, a line of high-tension towers stood ready, their arms akimbo like a dance line of steel kachinas waiting for the drums.

Beyond the little town, beyond the whitewashed church, beyond the weedy cemetery with it's sun-bleached crosses and faded plastic flowers, the road swung southeast, wound for a while along the sandy floodplain of the Chama River bottom, curved under the stern prow of Black Mesa and at San Juan Pueblo crossed the Rio Grande where children swam in the last of the clear water. Two miles farther downstream at Espanola, the silt-laden Chama joined the Rio Grande and from there, the color of the earth, it flowed like liquid adobe to the sea.

"You'll like this place we're going to stay," David said. Neither of them had spoken for an hour. It hadn't been necessary. "It's up in the hills behind town. Overlooks the valley. Wait till you see the view from the porch. One hundred and eighty degrees of pure space."

After Fuller had confirmed the appointment with Cowan, David had called an old friend in Santa Fe and arranged to stay overnight in his guest house.

"Sounds like my kind of place," Fuller said, slightly preoccupied.

"I'm sorry Ben and Judy won't be there," David said. "You would like them both. They're going to be away for the week but Ben said he would leave the key under the doormat."

Fuller twisted around to lean into the corner between the car seat and the door. "When McNutt testified at the first trial that he found a blue box at the campsite, what made him so sure that it belonged to Hammit?"

"What made you think of that?"

"I don't know. Just struck me as curious. What did he actually say?"

"He said it looked like a medicine box and he knew Hammit was taking medicine for his seizures."

"But why would he have made such an issue of it?"

"To establish Hammit's presence at the murder site?" David suggested.

"But by that time," Fuller argued, "Hammit had already admitted he was there. That he had walked up on Bell and the murdered men."

"Maybe McNutt was just playing with the minds of the jury. Trying to make linkages."

"Maybe so," Fuller said, crossing his arms. But he didn't seem satisfied. "Was the box introduced as evidence?"

"Not that I recall. Do you think McNutt made it up?"

Fuller let out a little sigh of exasperation. "You know, there's so much deception in this case, it's hard to know what to believe."

They drove through the highway town of Pojoaque and just before noon the road climbed and crossed the last of the juniper ridges that sloped rib-like off the limestone backbone of the Sangre de Cristos. At the bottom of the ridge the shallow river basin was crowded with the greens of cottonwoods and poplar and the adobe blocks of Santa Fe, tan and salmon buildings the color of the ground stacked like little pueblos, each repeating the tiered contours of the hills piled behind the town.

Built by the conquistadores along the northern reaches of the Camino Real, La Villa Real de San Francisco de Santa Fe was at the cultural and topographical crux of New Spain, the center point of two intersecting lines of Spanish settlements that lay along and across the valley of the Rio Grande from Taos to Tutahaco and from Pecos to the Pajarito Plateau like the beams of a fallen cross. For two and a half centuries this mission-fortress was the fulcrum of Spanish power in the New World. From here men did the bidding of the cardinals and the king. Spanish troops were quartered here the year Jamestown was born and a generation before the Pilgrims' first Thanksgiving, Franciscan friars were giving thanks in chapels already beamed and lit.

In five centuries since that first Catholic communion much about the little town has changed. The foreign flags have all come down, the soldiers marched away. The wagon trains have come and gone and cars now crowd the narrow streets where burros once carried water and wood. But from the ridge-top two miles away, it's hard to see these signs of change. From there this earthen city still resembles a seventeenth century adobe village and it is easy to imagine that within it there are still pointed ladders and painted pots, that on flat rooftops strips of meat hang drying in the sun, that women still sing over their metates and bronzed men trade turquoise for colored feathers in the dusty shade of the plaza.

David steered into the right lane and merged with the traffic headed down the hill into town. A low-rider pickup blared past, it's radio loud enough to bring rain. Propped atop the huge rubber tires the truck looked like a toy being carried away by a giant beetle.

They drove through town, past the park, to the upper end of East Alameda where they turned onto a dirt road.

"These Santa Feans love their dirt roads, don't they?" Fuller said.

"The City Different," David quoted.

The dirt road wound through chubby junipers for a hundred yards to the driveway of a large adobe house terraced up the hillside. David drove to the rear of the house and parked beside the porch of the guest quarters.

"Come with me. I'll show you to a great view," David said. He walked ahead to the porch then turning pointed to the west. "How about that?" he said. The valley, flat and perfectly level, stretched like a tight tan drumhead from under the weight of the hills where they stood to the angular, blue blocks of the Jemez Mountains twenty miles away. In the wide hard sky a thunderhead was building in the lee of Chicoma Peak. As they watched, the piled white tower, it's bright top sun-lit and beveled by the high altitude wind-shear, moved slowly off to the northeast trailing a gray veil of rain that reached almost to the ground.

"I want to stay here on the porch for a month or two," said Fuller, looking out over the valley.

"Just wait till sunset," David said. "Once you see that you will never leave."

"I don't want to already," Fuller said.

David unlocked the door and walked in. The sitting room floor was old Saltillo tile, most of it covered by a large Ganado rug. Between the peeled spruce ceiling beams latillas were arranged in a classic herringbone design. The plaster walls were painted white and in one corner was a rounded kiva fireplace, a row of red votive candles lined along it's curved mantle.

"Come on, pick your room," David said to Fuller. Carrying his suitcase, Fuller followed him through the house. More Navajo rugs hung on the walls. In every room, there were bookcases crowded with Acoma and Santa Clara pottery.

"Nice place, huh?" David said. "Makes you want to live in an adobe house."

"Yeah, I'll bet the guy who owns this place doesn't teach school," Fuller said sarcastically.

"He's what we called in Texas an independent oil operator."

"A wildcatter?"

"And a lucky one. Or a good one. Or maybe both. You should see the main house. He has a kachina collection that would make the Rockefellers and the Goldwaters envious. "

"Why don't I take this room?" Fuller said. "I like the bedspread."

"It's yours," David said. "Put your stuff down and I'll meet you on the porch."

*   *   *

"I spent a week here one summer," David said as they sat on the porch watching the clouds. "I came out to close the deal on a house." Fuller knew that what David could have said, but didn't, was that he and Susan had come out to close the deal.

"But," he stretched back in his chair and propped his feet on the corner of a low, tile table, "nothing ever came of it. At the last minute, the woman who owned it changed her mind and backed out of the deal. Just as well. I like it in Henson. The week I was here I spent most of my time sitting out on this porch."

"I can understand that," Fuller said.

"Some nights, you can hear coyotes in the hills."

"Sound human, don't they?"

"That's just what I thought the first time I heard them. I thought it was people imitating coyotes. What a serenade. Yelps and barks, choruses and blue notes. Sounds like part festival and part funeral."

"Probably a festival for the coyotes. A funeral for the rabbit."

"Maybe we'll hear them tonight. By the way, what time is it getting to be?"

Fuller glanced at his watch. "Two-thirty."

"We'd better go. We're due at Cowan's office at three."

"I can't move," Fuller groaned, theatrically "I'm paralyzed."

"Come on, old fellow," David said, pulling on Fuller's arm. "We'll be back in two hours."

*   *   *

Professor Cowan was a small man, tanned and balding. His gray hair was close cropped, military style, and a pair of glasses hung on a cord around his neck. He seemed pleased they had come.

"Thank you for seeing us so quickly," said Fuller.

"Well," Cowan said, locking his fingers together in front of him on the desk top, "your project is certainly an interesting one."

"As I indicated in the letter," Fuller said, sliding forward in his chair, "we are interested primarily in two things. First, how the five men with Hammit were killed, and second whether or not there was any cannibalism."

"Yes," said Cowan.

"Can you determine that" David asked, "whether or not there was cannibalism?"

"Well, sometimes we can," Cowan said thoughtfully. "But it depends. If the limbs were disarticulated, sometimes the joint surfaces are damaged in a characteristic way. Or if the flesh was cut from the long bones, the knife can leave longitudinal scratch marks or striations on the bones. Like this." Cowan rose from behind the desk, put on his glasses and selected a bone from several on the book shelf. Inspecting the bone as he walked, he crossed the small room to where David and Fuller sat, and held the bone out between them.

"This is a femur, a thigh bone," Cowan said. David and Fuller leaned to look. "If you look carefully here," he pointed to the shaft of the bone with a pencil, "you can see these marks, here and here, where the knife scraped the bone when the flesh was removed." Cowan looked over his glasses at the two men to satisfy himself that they were seeing the marks. "This happens to be the leg bone of a sheep," Cowan went on, "but the marks on a human bone would be the same." He handed it to Fuller who inspected it and then passed it to David.

"The marks are very characteristic when they are present, as you can see," Cowan said. He took the bone from David, placed it back on the shelf and sat back down behind the desk.

"Can you tell from examining a skeleton if someone was shot?' David asked.

"With a little luck," Cowan said. "If the bullet struck a bone, it might fracture it in a characteristic manner. Even if the bullet was deflected, traces of lead can be left on the bone. Traces of lead can be detected with x-rays."

David looked at Fuller. This was even better than he had expected.

"When would you be able to start?" Fuller said to Cowan.

"Well," he answered deliberately, "it's easier in the summer, of course. There are no classes, you see. And I would need some time for preparation. "

"Of course," David repeated.

"You have published a Notice of Exhumation?" Cowan said.

116

"Yes," said Fuller. "In the *Denver Post* last week."

"And the owner of the property where the graves are located?" Cowan asked. "Is he agreeable?"

"That's no problem," David said. "We have a letter from him here." David took a single sheet of paper from his briefcase and handed it across the desk. Cowan took the letter, tilted his head up to look through his glasses and read.

"Very thorough," Cowan said putting the letter carefully on the desk. "I like that." He smiled. "I would say we should be able to begin the excavation, let's say, within a month. Would that be satisfactory?"

"The sooner the better," said David, shifting forward in his chair.

"We have to wait thirty days after the publication of the exhumation notice," Fuller reminded him.

"I'll need to make a site visit," Cowan said thinking aloud, "perhaps in a week."

"You're welcome to stay at my place," David offered.

"Thank you, that's very kind," Cowan said, "but I have my own travel trailer. There are so many things to bring, you see."

"Of course," David said.

"Well," Cowan said. He pulled an appointment book toward him on the desk and opened it. "Let's see now. Why don't we say Wednesday, August 15th for the site visit," he made a note, "and" he paused again. "We will plan the excavation for September 1st. It shouldn't take more than one day." He looked up at the two men.

"Perfect," David said, trying to temper his excitement.

Cowan made another note.

"There will be a fee, of course," Fuller said.

"Oh, yes. The money." Cowan closed the date book and took off his glasses. He smiled benevolently. "Fortunately, we have some funds for projects like this. Grant money, you understand. I will want to report our findings, that is if we are successful."

"Of course," David said quickly.

"The university likes to see signs, periodically, that I am occupied." Cowan smiled.

"Is there anything else we need to do?" Fuller asked.

"I think not," Cowan said reassuringly. "Give me your address and your phone number and I will confirm all of this in a day or so. Oh, yes. I will need directions to the grave site."

David wrote out the information and handed it to Cowan who looked it over briefly and then stood up.

"Well, gentlemen," he said extending his hand across the desk to David, "it has been a pleasure. I look forward to our little adventure."

"Thank you very much," David said as they shook hands.

"Yes," Fuller added.

"Fine then," Cowan said. "I'll be seeing you soon."

*   *   *

"I like that guy," David said as they walked to the car.

"He does inspire confidence, doesn't he?"

"I hope he can help us," Fuller said, brushing his hand back over his greying widow's peak. It was a gesture he made often, especially when he was concerned.

"Well, he certainly sounds interested and Brewster sure gave him good marks."

"Oh, I think he's good," Fuller said. "I just hope there's something in that grave."

17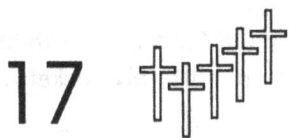

Sheriff Gibson stood hands on hips, his face screwed up with disgust. Fifty feet away two medics from the Search and Rescue team worked to free the burned body from the blackened wreckage. The sun directly overhead was heating the air in the rocky canyon and even at that distance, the stench was sickening. The jeep was so thoroughly burned and crushed from the impact that it was difficult to recognize but he was pretty sure it was Lomax's.

He hadn't seen the wrecked jeep on his way up the canyon. It was as he drove back down that he noticed the dirt broken away on the edge of the narrow road. When he stopped to look more closely, he spotted the burned wreckage in the rocks below.

It was Lomax's neighbor who had called. She had seen Lomax drive away from his house the morning after he arrived. When he did not come back that night she assumed he had gone to Gunther. But two days later when he still had not returned she thought that strange. Lomax had never come to town for just one day. On the third day she called the sheriff.

His jeep wasn't at the airport. The sheriff in Gunther had confirmed that. Neither had Lomax checked with his office in Houston. No one named Lomax had bought a plane ticket at the Gunther airport. The mine had been the first place the sheriff had checked.

The medics put what was left of him in a black body bag, slung it between them with ropes and started back up the rocky talus slope to the road. Sheriff Gibson walked over to the wreckage, and squatted down to think. On the ground near his feet, he noticed a wadded ball of newspaper, the edges partially burned. He picked it up and felt the weight of the rock inside. He unwrapped the partially burnt paper, noted that it was part of a page from the *Silver World*, and tossed it back on the ground. As he turned to leave that the glint caught his eye.

There, almost hidden among the rocks, was a small, round piece of metal. He picked it up and held it in the palm of his hand. It was a blue metal screw cap, three-quarters of an inch across. On the inside was a cork washer. It smelled of gasoline.

He put the cap in his pocket and stood for a minute thinking. Then he picked up the partially burned newspaper, put it in his pocket with the metal cap and started up the slope.

From his truck the sheriff watched the medics as they loaded Lomax's body into the van, then watched as they drove down the winding canyon road. But he didn't follow them immediately. He sat for a while thinking about the burned paper, turning the blue cap over and over in his hand. Suddenly he stopped short. He held the cap to his nose.

"Dammit!" he said out loud.

He got out of the truck and hurried back up the road to the spot where the jeep had gone over. For five minutes he walked slowly back along the road, periodically squatting down to inspect the gravel surface. Then he returned to his truck and drove to town. In his office, he made a long distance telephone call.

"No, sir," Sheriff Gibson said into the phone, "but there are a few peculiar things. Maybe you ought to send some of the boys from the crime lab out here."

He listened.

"No," he said, "it's pretty much burned up. I'm having the motor registration run down now, but I'm pretty sure it was his jeep."

He listened again.

"I'm not sure what time of day it was. Maybe nighttime but he knew that road pretty well. Yes, sir. Yes, sir. Well, for one thing, there weren't any skid marks on the road where the jeep went over. Right. Gravel. I would have expected to see something. Maybe his brakes failed? I know, it would be hard to tell now. Maybe the crime lab boys can help. Right. Right. Well, only one other thing. I never saw a wrecked car burned that bad. I mean, it's cooked, inside and out. Yes, it does seem funny, doesn't it? Maybe he did. He may have had extra gas cans with him. I did find a metal screw top. It looks like the top to a gas can. No, just the top. Outside the jeep. It hadn't been burned. I didn't find any gas cans. Could have been. No, sir, I'll be here all afternoon. Right, right. Tell him to call me here. Only one fellow. He lived at a cabin at the mine. Yes, he knew Lomax. He worked for him. I don't know. No one has seen him in a week."

18

"There appear to be five skeletons," Cowan said. He bent close over the luminous screen of the subsurface radar unit propped on the small dining table. With the shades drawn it was nearly dark inside the efficient space of the RV except for a glow from the luminous screen. David and Fuller and Dub, their lighted faces lined with concentration crowded behind Cowan, leaned over his khaki shoulders straining to make out the gray images on the small screen.

"Note the five separate pelvic bones," Cowan continued, pointing with the tip of a pencil. "And these long bones . . . femurs. Thigh bones."

"I'll be damned," Dub breathed, pushing his hat back on his forehead with his thumb.

"The bodies appear to have been lined up side by side," Cowan said, looking closely, adjusting the gain on the equipment, "but . . . one . . . two . . . three . . . four," he counted under his breath, "I see only four skulls."

"Just like McNutt said at the trial," David said. "He said Miller's skull was missing. McNutt was one of the original twenty-one men who left Utah," David explained to Cowan who was still studying the screen. "McNutt identified the five bodies after they were found by the survey crew."

"Ummm, yes," Cowan said, switching off the screen and turning to the men. "Well, gentlemen, there are indeed skeletons here. Shall we begin?"

The four men stepped down out of the RV and stood back as Cowan signaled for the radar unit to be moved away from the grave site. Satisfied, he nodded to the backhoe operator and the yellow machine's motor coughed to life.

A few men from town, drawn as much by the machinery as the history, had gathered to watch from behind the yellow tape Sheriff Gibson had stretched around the perimeter of the site.

"Fortunately, tourist season is over," David said to Fuller.

"And the wire services didn't pick up on the exhumation notice," Fuller added.

"We will take the soil off in layers," Cowan said over the noise of the backhoe, "and screen it all. Often, there are items of interest found around the burial site. For instance," he turned to David, "parts of the broken rifle."

The operator swung the metal bucket into position over the graves and with a final glance at Cowan gently carved away the first layer of topsoil, emptying it skillfully onto the screen frame. The two students who had come to assist Cowan, moved to the screen and brushed the dirt around over the screen as Cowan watched.

"The skeletons should be down about four feet according to the radar," Cowan said, leaning close to the men to be heard. "We will use the backhoe for the first three feet, and then switch to hand tools to avoid damaging any of the bones. They may be very fragile after all this time"

The operator poured another bucket full of dirt onto the screen and moved the arm, robot-like, back over the grave. David watched with admiration as the operator deftly manipulated the levers that gave life to the mechanical arm.

"That fellow could pick up a dime with that thing," Sheriff Gibson said to David when he saw him watching.

"Professor Cowan walked back and forth dividing his attention between the work of the backhoe and the two young men screening the dirt. Occasionally, he picked something from the screen, inspected it, and then tossed it away.

"The pH of the soil here is very favorable for the preservation of bones," Cowan said. "It's 6.5. Nearly neutral. That's good. Acid soil dissolves bones quickly. Leeches out the calcium."

Within an hour, the hole was three feet deep and Cowan motioned for the operator to stop. The students helped each other down into the hole and with Cowan watching began digging carefully with hand tools, putting the dirt into buckets which they passed up to be screened. It was 10:15 when the first bone was exposed. It was a skull, as Professor Cowan had predicted.

"Good, Jim," Cowan said. "Very careful now. Use the brushes," he coached. "We don't remove any of the bones until the entire grave site is exposed," Cowan said over his shoulder to the four men who had crowded up behind him. "It is important to record the position of the bones relative to each other. Sometimes that becomes very important later."

Working meticulously with small trowels and paint brushes the students removed the dirt bucket by bucket. Gradually, five full adult skeletons took form in the dirt. They lay by side, the bones of their marionette-like arms and legs angulated as if dumped in a show trunk, or arrested when the music stopped in the middle of a macabre dance step.

As the students worked, Cowan periodically took photographs and made drawings on a pad and talked quietly with the two young men.

"Gently now," Cowan said as one student handed up the first bone up to him. He took it in both hands, carried it carefully to a work table and placed it on a cloth. David and Fuller and Dub and the sheriff and the backhoe operator and the two students gathered around the table.

As a physician David had seen many bones, the clean articulated bones of the anatomical classroom models, always white, always smooth, like carved ash wood struts. Now, for the first time he was seeing bones as an historian. Brittle brown artifacts, stained and cracked, puzzle pieces, calcified clues that could solve a hundred-year-old mystery

"It's the femur of a grown man," Cowan said, brushing it gently with the soft-bristle brush. "See this bony ridge here?" he said pointing with the handle of the brush. "This is a muscle attachment. You are familiar with this," he said to David. "These ridges are much more prominent on men's bones due to the size and strength of the muscles."

He tied the string of a white paper tag around the bone and on the tag wrote 6/HE/B1/A/1.

"We are using the catalogue system developed by the Smithsonian," he explained as he wrote. "The first number is for the state. Colorado is the sixth state alphabetically. The HE is the county designation. B1 indicates this specimen came from burial site number one. I will use A for the first of the five individual skeletons, and 1 for the first bone of that skeleton."

He completed the tag and made an entry in a notebook.

Now," he said, "we will put each bone in a separate paper sack. The bones must not be allowed to dry in the sun. Drying too rapidly can cause them to crack. Then the sacks are placed in these cartons for transport. When we get them back to the school we will clean and stabilize them and examine them carefully. I must say, they are in excellent condition. Any defleshing marks should be easily apparent. Of course," he said looking at David," we will x-ray them also. That should help settle the gunshot question."

By four-thirty in the afternoon the bones of all five skeletons had been tagged and packed away. While the students loaded the cartons and the equipment the five men—David, Fuller, Dub, the sheriff and Professor Cowan—watched as the backhoe operator refilled the hole. The men from town drifted away in two's and three's.

"We will fill the hole for now," Cowan said. "Sheriff Gibson," he nodded toward the Sheriff, "thought it would be safer since it will be at least two weeks before our analysis is complete. After that, the bones can be reburied."

"You know," Dub said, "I've lived here all my life and I've always kinda' wondered if anyone was really buried here. I mean, the way stories get going and all."

"Well, thanks to you, Dub, "said David, "now we know."

"This has been very successful," Professor Cowan said.

"Now for the answers to the rest of the questions," David said.

"Cowan smiled. "The analysis should be very interesting, indeed."

"Each of the skulls was crushed, wasn't it?" David said to Cowan.

"It appears that way," Cowan said. "But it's not clear how they were crushed. We should be able to tell more from the microscopic examination."

"How will you identify the skeletons?" Fuller asked.

"Well," Cowan said, "some deductive reasoning will be required, of course, and we may never really know for sure. But we do know, for instance, that Noon was the youngest. Only eighteen, wasn't he?" he asked rhetorically. "And Swan was the oldest. Their skeletons should be easy enough to identify. My guess is that Swan is specimen B, but we shall see. Miller's skull was missing. Let's see. Noon, Swan, Miller. That leaves Humphreys and Bell. Separating those two might be more difficult."

"That will be easy," David offered, smiling. "Bell's skeleton will be the one with the bullet marks on the bones."

"Cowan laughed. "I hope we will be that lucky," he said.

One of the students appeared at Cowan's side. "We're all packed Professor."

"Well, gentlemen," Cowan said looking around at the four men. He put his hands on his knees and stood stiffly. "I've certainly enjoyed this day. I think we had best be going now. We have a long way to go."

"You and the students are certainly welcome to stay with us," David offered.

"Plenty of room," Dub added.

"Thank you," said Cowan. "That's very generous of you. So far we have eluded the press corps. I hate to push our luck. You know how fast word of this will travel. Tonight we will drive back as far as Alamosa. I have arranged for rooms there. By noon tomorrow we will be back at the school. As soon as I have finished with the examination, I will write you," Cowan said to David.

"Good," David said, "we will drive down and pick up the bones."

"We can review the results then," Cowan said. He turned to Dub. "Mr. Ponder . . . ."

"Dub," he interjected.

"Well, Dub, we are all certainly grateful to you, of course."

"I should be thanking you, Professor. Now I've really got some tales to tell."

David, Fuller and Dub watched as they drove away, the silver and tan RV angling up the steep approach to the pass until it was hidden by the trees. The sound of the laboring motor faded away leaving behind only the soft hiss of the river flowing nearby. David turned and stood looking at the grave.

"Kinda' spooky," Dub said, joining him, "digging up those bodies. It's like they were people you know."

"We do know them, sort of," David said. "At least we know quite a lot about them."

"Jolene is set on giving them a Christian burial, you know," Dub said. "She said everyone deserves a Christian burial, and she is sure they didn't get one before. She is planning to have a special service for 'em, the bones that is, when they are reburied."

"That's a nice idea," David responded.

"She's got it all planned," Dub continued. "She's already asked the Presbyterian minister to conduct the service."

"Why Presbyterian?" Fuller asked.

"He's our minister," Dub said. "Jolene said that since they weren't able to choose, she'd choose Presbyterian for 'em."

19 ✝✝✝✝✝

E rnest Soderholm fingered a pocket in his Donegal tweed waistcoat. A polished elk's tooth hung on a gold watch chain that lay in an arc from pocket to pocket across his buttoned front. From the pocket he produced a metal lighter and, turning it upside down, thoroughly lit his pipe, rhythmically puffing out a slow smoke signal. Inspecting the pipe carefully and satisfying himself that it was properly lit, he held it aside, the tip of the mouthpiece just touching his lips, and looked across the large desk at David and Fuller as if to signal he was ready to begin.

"It's a very interesting episode," Soderholm said thoughtfully, "this Hammit affair." The old man was from another time. His hair was perfectly white, except for a pale yellow tint in the wave over his forehead. His full walrus mustache matched his hair. Even in the warmth of the Denver summer morning, he seemed comfortable in the stiff white collar and wool suit. Framed by the single leaded glass window behind him, he was as much a fixture of the dark-paneled Victorian library as the mahogany desk or the brass lamps or the heavily mantled fireplace or the cracked, old-shoe men's-club comfort of the burgundy leather sofa. He was perfectly suited to his environment which might have been created for him—a museum diorama, a sepia photograph, a zoo habitat specifically designed for an endangered species. It was easy to imagine him, hands clasped behind his back, walking the shaded street in front of his turreted brownstone mansion or meticulously tending his flower garden.

"My great-grandfather met Hammit, you know," he said proudly, adjusting his glasses and examining the two men across the desk from him. "He was present at Hammit's second trial. In Gunther." The old man spoke slowly, punctuating his sentences with smoky puffs. During the pauses Fuller and David waited politely.

"We were told your great-grandfather had quite an interest in the Hammit case," David said encouraging him, "and that he was responsible for Hammit's pardon."

126

"I think that's fair to say," Soderholm agreed. "He was quite a historian as well, you know. He kept a diary every day from January 1,1867, until May 27, 1910, two days before his death. Eleven volumes." He gestured, pistol-like, with the stem of his pipe toward the bookshelf beside the fireplace. "I hope to see it published someday if this old frame holds out. But," he said turning back toward the two men, "it's Hammit you gentlemen are interested in." His mouth was hidden beneath his moustache, but behind gold rimmed glasses, the lines at the corners of his eyes suggested he was amused, and about to smile. "How can I be helpful?"

"Well," David said, "We thought it might be interesting, after all this time, to review what is known about the Hammit case. From a historical point of view." David found himself instinctively talking loudly, a habit acquired during his medical practice to avoid embarrassing older patients who might be hard of hearing. "We learned of your great-grandfather's interest in the case and . . . ."

"You are going to dig up the bodies," Soderholm finished the sentence unexpectedly. David glanced at Fuller. "I saw the exhumation notice in the paper," Soderholm explained, smiling. Then as an afterthought, "It won't help any, you know."

"Well," David began, "we thought perhaps examining the bones might give some new clues."

"It might," Soderholm said, matter-of-factly, "but I doubt it. What you are really trying to do, of course, is to determine whether or not Hammit was guilty. Isn't that right?" He brushed some ashes on the desk top into a pile, pinched it and dropped it into an ashtray.

"Well . . . yes," said David.

"Then you have come to the right place," Soderholm said. Fuller and David exchanged glances. "You must have noticed in your research that there were some people, quite familiar with the case, who were not called as witnesses at the trials?"

"Yes," said Fuller. "Otto Meers for one."

"Yes, he's an obvious one," Soderholm agreed, "but there were also Pounds and Morey and Laughton." He took the pipe from his mouth and blew a thin stream of smoke at the ceiling. "My great-grandfather was curious about that as well. That is why he interviewed these men."

"We were told that he did," Fuller said.

"Yes, well, he interviewed them in 1889, three years after the second trial. He found Gabe Pounds living in Basalt near Glenwood Springs. Pounds, you will recall, had been in the original party of twenty-one men who left Utah for Breckenridge. He told my great-grandfather that all the men in the party were strangers to him when he joined them. Just before they set out from Utah Hammit came into the camp and asked if he could go along. He said he was broke and had no money to pay his passage but that he would help with the horses. He also said he had lived in Colorado and knew the country and that he could be useful as a guide. Pounds described Hammit as a strong robust young man with the appearance of an athlete."

"Pounds said that the first night out Hammit had a fit and fell into the fire. Pounds dragged him out. From then on until they came to Ouray's camp Hammit had the fits regularly. Apparently, most of the other men in the company didn't want Hammit around and asked Pounds to drive him away. But Pounds said he told them Hammit did his part and behaved as well as any of the rest and had as much right as any of them to go along. He said he had no reason to be afraid of being around Hammit."

David remembered that McGrue had also befriended Hammit, at times holding him when he had the seizures.

"But," Soderholm continued, "the other men in the group hated Hammit and were hard on him. Pounds said he never knew exactly why. He remarked that Hammit was quiet and never quarreled with any of them. In fact, he generally avoided the other men, eating alone perhaps because he knew they didn't like him.

David and Fuller waited while Soderholm coughed and cleared his throat. "In January," Soderholm went on, "the party reached Ouray's camp where they waited for two or three weeks. Ouray had advised them they could not get through the mountains because of the deep snow. But Swan and Miller and Bell and Humphreys became bored and impatient and determined to go on. Ouray told them they would be found dead in the snow."

All but one of them, David thought.

"Pounds said he never knew if Hammit asked these men if he could go along with them but he was with them when they left Ouray's camp. They had guns and could have driven him back but they didn't. Pounds said the next time he saw Hammit was at the Indian Agency."

David shifted in his seat. "Pound's party followed Hammit's party to the Agency?"

"Yes," replied Soderholm. "They arrived at the Agency about a month after Hammit, but left again within a day or so to prospect down around Antelope

Park. Pounds said he was camped there when he heard the five bodies had been found over near Henson. Pounds said the word was Hammit had killed them to rob them. That surprised Pounds. He never knew the men had any money with them. He assumed that they had money for necessities, enough to get started prospecting, but no one was rich. At least not that he ever heard of. Pounds said he was privy to rumors about the money Hammit was supposed to have taken from them, but on the entire trip he never heard of it or saw any of it."

"You said most of the men hated Hammit from the start?" Fuller asked.

"According to Pounds," Soderholm replied.

"And Hammit hated them?" David asked.

Soderholm took a long pull on his pipe and blew the smoke slowly to one side before answering. "Wouldn't you?"

David shifted uneasily in his chair.

"Who was Morey?" Fuller asked Soderholm.

"Sean Morey was with the men who buried the bodies after they were found by the crew working on the toll road. He had gone into the Henson Valley with a group of prospectors in May. A month later they were camped at Acme Creek when an artist from Harper's magazine came into camp and told them five bodies had been found down near the river. Morey and the other men went down to see. By then McNutt had come over from Saguache to identify the bodies. Morey said the smell was horrible, and that he didn't get close but he could see four of the bodies lined up together partially covered with blankets. The fifth body was off quite a way from the others and the head was missing. Some of the other men helped bury the bodies and brought some guns and other relics back to the camp. There was a lot of talk about the bodies and the condition they were in. The men argued about whether or not Hammit had eaten the bodies but they all agreed Hammit probably had killed them since he was the only one left alive."

"Did you say guns?" David said.

"Yes. He used the plural," Soderholm said.

"Was there any money on the bodies?" Fuller asked.

"Morey said that he didn't remember any talk of money."

"But he was clear about one of the heads being missing?" David said.

"Yes. He said the bodies were intact," Soderholm confirmed. No limbs were missing. Only the head of the body that lay off from the rest."

"And Laughton?" Fuller said. "Who was Laughton?'

Soderholm leaned back in his chair and pulled slowly at one side of his moustache. "James Laughton was a prospector who was with Baker when he made the first discoveries over at Silverdale. When the pay played out, he moved to Saguache in 1870. He was one of the viewers hired by Meers to lay out the road from Saguache top Silverdale."

"Viewers?" David asked.

"What you call a surveyor now," Soderholm replied. "He worked for Meers. On the toll road. Laughton and Hoskiss and a man named Bartolf, started out early in April from Saquache working southwest toward the headwaters of Los Alamos Creek staking out the grades for the roadway. He said because of the snow and ice still on the ground in the high country at that time of year they had the horses roughshod. They traveled several days viewing out, as he put it, the course they thought the road should take across the divide to the Lake Fork of the Gunther River then up the river and on over into Burrough's Park. During the trip they blazed trees with axes and cut brush. Laughton said that with all this clearing plus the tracks of the roughshod horses on the mud and snow, they left a wide trail a blind man could follow."

"On their way back to Saguache they camped near the lower end of Crystal Lake along the river at the foot of what is now called Cannibal Plateau. The next morning Laughton went down to the river where he discovered what appeared to be an abandoned campsite. In the trees by the river someone had built a bark lean-to and Laughton said that from the amount of ashes in the fire pit it appeared that whoever had built the camp had kept a fire for a long time. Inside the lean-to was a depression in the bare ground as though someone had laid in it in one position for a long time. There were indentations for his head, shoulders and hips and oblong marks where his feet would have been. Laughton even said it appeared to him that whoever had lain there had been in some sort of delirium, repeatedly pulling his feet up and back, scooping out two holes with his heels."

"He didn't see the bodies?" David asked.

"No," Soderholm said. "They weren't found until later. At another campsite nearby. The camp Laughton found was apparently a hundred yards or so from the campsite where the bodies were found. Laughton said he looked around but found only pieces of blanket he said looked worn as if they had been used for shoes. He found no sign of game. No bones or fur or hides and said he wondered at the time what the man had lived on."

"When Laughton returned to the Agency he talked freely about the campsite. Within a few days Hammit came to him and questioned him about the campsite, but Laughton said afterwards he was in doubt as to whether Hammit knew the place or not."

"It must have been Hammit's camp," David said.

"Almost certainly," Soderholm agreed.

"That accounts for McNutt's testimony," David said to Fuller. "He said the fire at the camp where the bodies were found was small and it didn't look as if they had camped there long. Hammit must have moved to that other campsite after the men were killed."

"But," said Fuller, getting back to an earlier point, "if Laughton and the other men had left a trail from the Agency back toward the campsites that easy to follow it's hard to believe Hammit could get lost like McNutt said he did when they took Hammit back to try to find the bodies."

"Precisely," Soderholm said. " And that question came up at the second trial, didn't it? That's why my great-grandfather sought out James Downs."

At the sound of that name David and Fuller shot glances at each other. "Downs was the Justice of the Peace at the Agency and he was with McNutt and the other men who took Hammit back up into the mountains to try to find the bodies. At the first trial, you will recall, McNutt testified that when they left the Agency they went up Los Alamos Creek to the Divide. That would have been along the course marked out by Laughton and the survey party.

"However," Soderholm went on, "Downs told my great-grandfather that on the backtrack they didn't go up Los Alamos Creek at all. Downs said Hammit led them straight to the Divide, keeping well north of Los Alamos Creek to a large park covered with downed timber. Hammit told them that he had been there but that the timber must have been covered with snow and said that if they went on up to the top of the mountain he might be able to get his bearings. At that point the men thought Hammit was lying and returned to the Agency."

"So, according to Downs," David said, leaning forward, "the backtrack party didn't follow Laughton's trail up Los Alamos Creek at all?"

"No," said Soderholm. "If they had they would have come to the Gunther River well south of the campsite where the bodies were found. Downs said later that the downed timber Hammit led them to was on a high ridge that divided the drainage of the Cebolla Creek and the Lake Fork and that if they had continued to the top of the ridge as Hammit suggested they would have been able to see the lake and the campsite."

"So Hammit wasn't lying and he wasn't lost. He was leading them almost on a direct line to the bodies," David said.

"Mmmm," Soderholm nodded.

"And," Fuller added, "that's why at the trial Hammit said that Downs could clear it all up?" Fuller added.

"Exactly!" said David

Soderholm smiled.

"Why would McNutt lie about going up Los Alamos Creek?"

"Well," Soderholm said, "remember McNutt didn't think much of Hammit. Maybe he was too quick to believe Hammit was guilty."

"Or too quick to see him convicted," David said.

Fuller turned to Soderholm. "You said your great-grandfather helped Hammit obtain his pardon. How did that happen?"

"That's a long story too," Soderholm said and, as if in preparation, he took a small metal tool from his pocket and began tamping gently at the bowl of his pipe. "Sometime after Hammit was sent to prison," he said as he worked, "he filed an appeal but ran out of money and couldn't pursue it. He passed his time carving canes and making watch fobs from horsehair." He folded the pipe tool, put the pipe in the ashtray and swiveled his chair to face the bookshelf. "I have one of them here." Soderholm stood stiffly and eased to the bookshelf. He moved to the sofa where David and Fuller were seated examining the watch fob as he walked. He held it out to David. "Hammit gave this to my great-grandfather."

David took the fob from Soderholm and held it so Fuller could see it. Four inches long and half an inch wide, the tightly braided fob was made of interlocking cords of black and russet horsehair. Attached to one end was a small ring and on the other a tiny horseshoe fashioned from a piece of metal. David handed it back to Soderholm who walked around the desk where he sat down.

"Hammit sold these," said Soderholm, placing the fob on the desk in front of him, "and the canes and the belts. He was given a plot of ground where he raised flowers which he also sold. It wasn't long before he had the money to finance another appeal but that was denied. You are doubtlessly familiar with that travesty?"

"Yes," said David. "He hadn't appealed the verdict immediately after the trial so no record was prepared. When he did appeal, it was denied because there was no record of the trial proceedings to review."

"Yes," said Soderholm, pleasantly surprised at David's familiarity with the details "Well," he continued, "Hammit soon gave up on the idea of an appeal and began to apply for pardon. Several petitions for pardon were denied. That's when my great-grandfather decided to act."

Soderholm retrieved his pipe from the ashtray where he had set it and began filling it from a glass canister on the desk, talking slowly as he worked. "My grandfather was a very meticulous man. He prepared a fourteen page statement detailing the history of the affair as he knew it, including his first-hand account of the trial at Gunther, summaries of the interviews of the four men who were not called to testify at the trial and a reasoned analysis of the legal proceedings, the denied appeal and the rejected applications for pardon. He drew three conclusions which he said would convince all but the most prejudiced minds."

Having finished with the pipe Soderholm set it aside, folded his hands and looked across the desk at David and Fuller.

"Yes . . . well," Soderholm said, clearing his throat. "First, as the result of the seizures Hammit may have suffered from a decadence of the brain which, coupled with the starving and the cold and the worry, brought on an insanity which led to the murders. If so, he was not guilty. Second, Hammit knowing they were surely going to die of starvation and that the other men in the party hated him and would have killed him to survive, may have killed the other men to preserve his own life. If so, he was not guilty. And third, it is possible that Hammit told the truth when he said that the crazed Bell killed the other men and then attacked him. If so, he was not guilty."

David and Fuller sat fascinated.

"My grandfather studied this matter for twenty-six years and was convinced that the unfortunate Hammit was not a premeditated murderer and that he should be pardoned."

"What did he do with the statement?" Fuller said.

"On January 2, 1901, he delivered the statement to the editor of the *Rocky Mountain Press* and the next day the paper printed the entire text under the headline, "Justice Fails: Innocent Man Kept Behind Bars For Seventeen Years". A companion article under the byline of Roman True charged that Otto Meers, through his influence with the governor, was directly responsible for the pardon denials. According to True, Meers feared Hammit because of threats Hammit had made during the second trial and he was determined to see that Hammit stayed in prison."

"What a story!" David exclaimed.

"Go on" Fuller urged.

"Hammit, of course, immediately applied again for a pardon," Soderholm said.

"Perfect!" said Fuller.

"But Meers . . . ." David began.

"Meers, you must know," Soderholm stressed, "was a very influential man in Colorado at that time. He had become very wealthy from his toll roads and railroads and the town sites he developed and while he never sought a public office for himself he was the acknowledged kingmaker of the Republican party in the state. It was said a governor could not be chosen without his consent. Meers was chairman of the board that planned and built the capitol building and after construction the legislature voted to hang his portrait permanently on the front wall of the Senate Chamber."

"It's still there," David said.

"It is not clear, however," Soderholm went on, "whether the newspaper's interest in Hammit was motivated by a desire to see justice done or to embarrass Governor Thompson who was planning to run for the US Senate. But the article created a sensational response. Petitions demanding Hammit's pardon flooded into the governor's office from all over the state. The governor refused to be interviewed and Meers came running."

"Meers surfaced?" said David.

"Yes," said Soderholm. "At the time he was in Washington engaged in construction of the Chesapeake Railroad. Within three days after the newspaper printed the story Meers was in Denver where he had a private meeting with the governor. In the statement released to the newspaper Meers again recounted seeing the Wells Fargo note in Hammit's wallet and reinforced his denial that he played any part in Hammit's escape from jail in Saguache. He accused Hammit of lying about becoming lost after leaving Ouray's camp and about Bell's role in the murders. In concluding the statement, Meers said he had come to Denver to discuss the affair at the governor's request and denied any intent to interfere with Hammit's application for pardon."

"Here we go again," Fuller said sarcastically.

"Meers," said Soderholm, "also quoted from a letter he said he received the day before from Charles Adams."

"The Adams who testified at the trial?" Fuller said.

"Yes," replied Soderholm. "In the letter Adams referred to threats Hammit made against him and Meers and Judge Gerry at the conclusion of the second trial, noting that Hammit said he would not only kill these men but would also take out his vengeance on their families. Referring to Adams in particular, Hammit was quoted to have said that he would take special pleasure in eating a piece of his—Adams'—flesh."

"Whoa!" David moaned.

"As you might expect," Soderholm said, "shortly after Meers' visit, the governor again refused Hammit's appeal for pardon."

"But," David said troubled, "I thought you said your great-grandfather . . . ."

" . . . was influential in securing Hammit's pardon?" Soderholm finished his sentence.

"Yes"

"There's more," Soderholm said shifting his weight in his chair. "On January 13, two days after the pardon was denied events took a strange turn. William Anderson, a prominent Denver attorney, who had long been interested in the Hammit trial, went to the offices of the *Rocky Mountain Press*. Anderson had spent some time studying the legal proceedings, and held the view that the crime had been committed on Indian territory and that Colorado law had no jurisdiction in the case. The paper's editor and legal counsel were interested, another meeting was arranged and Anderson was instructed in the interim not to accept any money from Hammit or make any arrangement for his defense."

David frowned, confused.

"Early the next morning," Soderholm continued, "Anderson went to the prison where he met with Hammit for two hours. When he left Anderson had $25 and Hammit's power of attorney. On learning of this development the editor became incensed and contacted Anderson, demanding he come to the editorial office the next morning. At the meeting, a violent argument broke out and a struggle followed during which Anderson shot and wounded the editor in the leg."

David and Fuller shook their heads in exasperation.

"Anderson was arrested, charged with assault with a dangerous weapon and his trial was set for April 23. As you can imagine the trial was the talk of the state, especially when it became known that Alfred Hammit would testify as a witness for the prosecution."

"We should have come here in the beginning," David said to Fuller.

Soderholm looked pleased. "On the first day of the trial Hammit, in his first public appearance in seventeen years, took the stand before a jam-packed courtroom. They came for miles to see the Colorado Cannibal, the Man-Eating Murderer, the Fiendish Ghoul. But during his testimony and the subsequent cross-examination Hammit was calm and reserved. He spoke in a strong clear voice without hesitation, answering the questions which were put to him thoughtfully and diffidently. At one point he corrected the cross-examiner politely and added some information which the attorney had omitted, a gesture that brought a smile from the judge. The spectators sat spellbound. This was not at all what they expected."

Soderholm got up and walked slowly to the window where he stood for a moment looking out at the shaded street. Then he turned to face the two men. "The trial lasted only one day. Anderson was convicted and given a suspended sentence. But it was Hammit's courtroom performance that captured the attention of the people and the press. The editorial pages were filled with wonder that this quiet man, misjudged and persecuted, could have ever been so awfully wronged or silenced so long."

"Following the trial Hammit, unmanacled, was given a day-long tour of the city and was everywhere met with smiles. In the streets people pressed around him in crowds wishing him a prompt release from prison. He was given a ride in an automobile, on a streetcar, on an elevator. He ate ice cream. And at the end of the day he returned to prison. The next morning, April 25, 1901, in his last official act as governor, Thompson granted Alfred Hammit his parole."

David and Fuller, realizing they had been sitting forward with anticipation, leaned back in the sofa.

"So you see, gentlemen," Soderholm said returning to his chair, "it is likely great-grandfather helped free Alfred Hammit. At least, I like to think so." He folded his hands across his vest

"What finally happened to Hammit?" David said.

"Well," Soderholm said solemnly, "it's rather sad I'm afraid. After his release, he went to live in Deer Creek Canyon near a family who befriended him. He kept to himself, tending his small flower garden and taking long walks. A year later he was found unconscious, perhaps from an epileptic attack. He was taken to the home of a neighbor where he died later that day. Before he died he regained consciousness and, sensing death, related to the neighbors at the bedside the sad events in the San Juans. It was the story he had told at his trial twenty-seven years earlier and the story he had, ever since that day, insisted was the truth."

For a while none of the men spoke. David and Fuller sat on the sofa thinking. Soderholm turned his chair to face the bookshelf and elbows on the chair arms, put his spread fingertips together in front of his face.

"You have been very helpful," Fuller said, breaking the uneasy silence. Soderholm turned to face them.

"It was a tragic affair," he said. Then after a pause, "When do you expect to exhume the bodies?"

David and Fuller exchanged a quick glance. "Actually, it's already done," Fuller said. "We expect to hear from the anthropologist anytime. Perhaps by the time we get home we will have some word. I'll be sure to send you a copy of his report."

Soderholm smiled, knowingly. "I would be very interested in his findings."

"Would it be possible," Fuller asked, hesitantly, "to see your great-grandfather's diary?"

Soderholm studied Fuller across the desk and then, as if to signal it was time for the interview to end, stood and walked around his desk. "Well, he began, "someday perhaps. Of course you are welcome to use whatever you want of what I have told you here today but I think I had rather leave it at that for now. I'm sure you understand."

"Of course," David said as they got up.

"Thank you again," David said to Soderholm. The three shook hands. David and Fuller walked toward the door, Soderholm between and slightly behind, one of his hands paternally on each of their shoulders.

"Have you been to the grave site?" Soderholm asked as they stopped at the door. "It's very near here you know. I think you might find it interesting."

"That's our next stop," said Fuller.

"I've enjoyed out talk gentlemen," Soderholm said. He seemed sincere. "I wish you luck on your project."

David and Fuller thanked Soderholm again and left.

*   *   *

The identical government-issue headstones, like buff-colored soldiers in a close order formation, stood spaced with stiff, military precision on the close-clipped green of the small cemetery. It took David and Fuller twenty minutes to locate the marker. Arched across the face of the stone in raised block letters was the name of the dead soldier, Alfred G. Hammit. Beneath the name, the letters spelled out Co. F, 16 US INF.

Inside the cemetery office the entry in the registration book indicated that Alfred Hammit had been buried on April 24, 1911. Officers of the James M.

Hawthorne Post No. 83, G.A.R. conducted the services. Fuller traced the entry with his finger and then turned to David.

"Look at this," he said pointing. David leaned to see. In the space after next of kin was marked, Uncle Sam.

20 †††††

David accelerated smoothly up the ramp onto the westbound lanes of I-70. It was early Sunday morning and the Denver traffic was light. A cold wave had passed through in the night clearing the air and ahead of them, completely filling their windshield, the front range of the Rockies stood out in stenciled relief against the pure sky.

David took a sip of coffee, propped his cup back on the dashboard and laughed quietly to himself.

"What's so funny?" Fuller said.

"I never eat or drink in a car that I don't think of a Nigerian taxi driver I had in Washington D. C. once. When he stopped for me up, he had just returned from taking his mother to the airport. She was seventy years old, and had never been out of Nigeria. Before she boarded the plane, she told him he should return to Nigeria with her, that America was no place for her son. 'In America,' she said, 'the people are savages. They eat and drink in their cars.'"

"That's Western civilization for you," Fuller said, laughing.

Skirting the downtown buildings, David turned south along Highway 25, and at its intersection with 287 turned right and headed west into the mountains. This route back to Henson took an hour longer than the flat route through Walsenburg and across the Antonio Valley but David didn't need to ask Fuller which he preferred. The mountains were a strong attraction for both men. It was one of their shared bonds. Being in the mountains was as important for them as being near the sea was for others. It was the preposition that was important. Being in the mountains meant being surrounded by the mountains, physically and spiritually, dominated by their presence and their majesty, pleased by their infinite variety and confronted by feelings of personal insignificance and vulnerability, as if summoned to the court of a powerful and magnificent monarch.

Beyond the strip malls and the condos the road narrowed to two lanes, crossed through the neatly stratified layer-cake geology of the hog back road cut and began its winding climb up Turkey Creek Canyon. David leaned back stretching his arms against the steering wheel.

"Well," said Fuller, "what did you think of Soderholm?"

"He certainly made Hammit seem more likable didn't he?"

"And more of a victim," Fuller added.

"It's ironic isn't it, considering his disastrous behavior at his own trial, that it may have been Hammit's courtroom performance in Denver that secured his freedom."

"Mmmmm," Fuller agreed

"I must say, "David said, "Soderholm convinced me Hammit wasn't lying about being lost when the men at the Agency took him back to find the bodies. It makes you wonder if Hammit wasn't telling the truth about the other things he was accused of lying about."

"Like the Wells Fargo note?"

"That, and his contention that Meers gave him the key to the jail and told him to escape. Maybe even helped him."

"Well, from what we've learned so far, it seems pretty clear that whether or not Hammit was guilty, he certainly got a raw deal from the legal system. There is no way he could have gotten a fair trial in Henson, or Gunther for that matter, and that Catch-22 about the trial records and the appeal is a joke!"

"And what about being tried on five different counts of manslaughter simultaneously," David added. "Even if he was guilty, the most he should have served was eight years and with good behavior he probably would have been out in three."

"Not as long as Meers had anything to say about it."

"Meers really seemed afraid of Hammit, didn't he?" said David.

"Well, if there was any one who cinched Hammit's conviction it was Meers. Giving Hammit the key to the jail, if he did, and telling him to run made Hammit a fugitive and essentially sealed his guilt. And Meers' story about the Wells Fargo note made money the motive. Straightforward robbery and murder."

"Right," David agreed. "And when Hammit accused Meers of lying about the key and the Wells Fargo note, it was Hammit's word against Meers and by not showing up at the second trial Meers avoided any further cross-examination."

"And then, after the conviction," said Fuller, "Meers used his influence with the governor to make sure Hammit's appeals for parole were denied. It wouldn't surprise me if Meers had something to do with the fact that there were no records of that second trial."

"So," said David, "Meers lied to have Hammit convicted, he made sure there were no records available from the second trial so there could be no appeal, and he corrupted the parole process to assure that Hammit remained in prison."

"He probably thought Hammit was just crazy enough to kill him, especially after the threats Hammit made at the trial."

"But he was wrong," David said.

"Maybe he wasn't. Maybe Hammit was just in prison long enough to get over it."

Talking as they drove, David and Fuller continued up the gentle wedge of the Platte River valley and just before noon crossed the timbered summit of Kenosha Pass. David pulled over and stopped alongside the guard rail. A thousand feet below them, the tawny grassland of South Park lay stretched out flat under the sky. Mountains bordered the sunken park—the Mosquito Range to the west, the Front Range to the east—and curving gently toward each other met at the horizon where, faded by the distance, they closed a pastel circle eighty miles across. In the sky between the mountains as if supported on an invisible pane scalloped cumulus clouds, all their flat lavender bottoms at the same altitude, floated over the valley like blossoms on a glass-topped table.

"I wish Russey Gott could see this," David said.

Fuller didn't recognize the name from any of David's previous stories.

"He was my neighbor in New Hampshire. He worked all his life in the woods. Seventy years old and he had never been out of the state. One day he came over to the house to tell me he was going out west to visit. Great, Russey. Where are you going? 'Out to Connecticut,' he answered."

"What did you say?"

"I can't remember now, but I was very disappointed. I was hoping he could come out here. To see places like this."

David smiled. "Good ol' Russey. I took him to the airport and when he boarded the plane he still had his gum-rubber boots on."

"Out to Connecticut," Fuller repeated, shaking his head.

"One day just before he died Russey and his wife showed up at my office. I was surprised to see them. He had never complained of any illness that I knew of, but I was worried it was something serious when they came in together. When I asked him what was wrong his wife spoke for him. I saw that a lot. The wife speaking for the husband when he was sick. As if he's somehow reluctant to admit any weakness. Especially illness. It was clear she didn't want to embarrass him, but was willing to do what she could to help him get the care she was afraid he needed."

"'Russey's been feeling kinda' unnecessary,' she said."

"It took some time for me to realize she was trying to tell me Russey was depressed."

"'Tell him, Russey,' she said, putting her hand on his knee. He sat there with his hands folded, looking at the floor.

"'Well, Doc,' he said, 'we've plum run out of children.'"

"I knew his youngest had just left home to try to get work in Massachusetts but I hadn't realized how symbolic that was for Russey. It was clear it was hard for him to talk about it."

"'For all those years, he said, it was ding-dong this, ding-dong that. Now there's nobody wants anything. You know, Doc, I don't know whether it's worse to be ding-donged to death or not needed.'"

"I guess some people are more fragile than they seem?" David winced inside and glanced to see if he had offended Fuller. If so he didn't let on.

*   *   *

Beyond the summit the road angled down off the pass in a wide sweeping curve descending gracefully into the broad basin. At the bottom of the hill a road branched off to the right into the mountains. David noted the road sign as they passed. BRECKENRIDGE 46 MILES.

Bearing to the left they drove south along the grassy flank of the Mosquito Range. Horses grazed on the manila hills and black and white magpies, flushed by the car noise, blew across the road, barred wings beating an urgent semaphore. David shifted his weight in the seat and stretched. The hot spot under his left shoulder blade was bothering him as it always did on long drives and he dropped his hand from the wheel and hung his arm down beside the seat to relax it.

An approaching car passed, headed north, and David watched in the rear view mirror as it turned off toward Breckenridge. Over that same bright plan in the lee of those same mountains but for one wrong turn, Alfred Hammit and his five companions would have walked one spring morning, bound, too, for Breckenridge and promise, and another new start.

At Antero they turned west crossing through the mountains at Trout Creek Pass into the valley of the Arkansas River. From there it was two hours to Henson.

It was 6:15 when David pulled up in front of the Pine Cone Cafe. Dub, who had seen them drive up, met them at the door breathless with excitement.

"By golly, you boys missed out on the happenings." Before they could ask what it was, Dub blurted out, "Lomax is dead!"

"Dead?" said David, startled

"Dead," Dub repeated. "Found his body burnt to a crisp in the canyon just below the Golden Fleece."

"Did you say burned?" David confirmed.

"Cooked!" said Dub. "Him and the jeep. He went off the road right at the steepest place. Right at the head of the creek. Must be five hundred feet to the bottom of the canyon. Looked like it exploded when it hit bottom. Sheriff had to get the Search and Rescue squad over from Gunther to get the body out. They just left. You must have passed them on the road."

"When did it happen?" Fuller asked

"They just found the wreck yesterday," Dub said, his small eyes as wide as they could stretch. "But they figure it musta' happened last week."

David, puzzled, pulled out a chair and sat down.

"I drove up to the canyon to see for myself," Dub continued as he and Fuller sat down at the table with David. "Hell, everybody in Henson was there."

"What happened?" David asked.

"They don't know for sure," Dub said. "Sheriff ain't talkin much about it but personally I think that sorry Lott kid had something to do with it."

"What does Sonny say?" Fuller asked.

"They can't find him," Dub said. "Nobody's seen him in a week. Looks like he disappeared just about the time it happened. Faye Johnson said Lomax drove in late last Thursday night. Next morning he left at dawn and never came back. She got worried and called Sheriff Gibson. He's the one who found the wreck."

Dub caught his breath. "I told you that little sumbitch was no good."

"What do you make of that?" David said to Fuller.

Dub, anxious to continue his story, went on. "Sheriff did say one thing."

"What's that?" asked David.

"He said when he got up to the mine Sonny's pickup was gone, but the dump truck was still there, loaded up and ready to go. He said there was a big pile of high grade ore right outside the entrance to the mine. Sheriff said he thought at the time that if Sonny was loadin' up for a trip to the smelter it was funny he would leave all that high-grade behind."

"Of course!" said David. "That explains the nighttime trips!" One quick look told him the same idea had dawned on Fuller.

Dub sat forward interested.

"We never told you about following Sonny, did we?" David said to Dub.

"Followed him where?" Dub said.

"Well," David began, "one night we were fishing down below town and Sonny drove by in his pickup just about dark. After what you had said about running drugs we decided to follow him to see where he was going. We followed him to the crossroads at Gunther but he didn't go to Gunther. He turned off and headed toward Montrose."

"See there." Dub said, pushing his hat back on his head. "I knew he wasn't going to Gunther to see no girlfriend."

"The next morning," David continued, "I got up early and sat in the park, waiting. Just after dawn Sonny drove by. He came in from the north and headed through town up toward the mine. He had been somewhere all night. Considering the length of time he had been gone, if he averaged fifty-five miles an hour he could have made a round trip of nearly five hundred miles."

Dub frowned, thinking.

"A week later we followed him again," David said. "This time we went to the crossroads and waited for him. When he came by we followed him all the way to Montrose."

"Montrose?" Dub said.

"But he didn't stop there," David said. "He went right on through town and west on I-70."

"To the smelter in Salt Lake!" Dub exclaimed.

"I don't know," David said. "We quit following him in Montrose."

"By Golly, that's it!" He pounded his palm smartly with his fist. "He was headed to the smelter," Dub said, convinced. "Sheriff was right. Was the pickup loaded?"

"You know, I don't remember." David looked at Fuller who shrugged. "It could have been but I wasn't thinking about that at the time so I didn't notice."

"I'll bet that's what it was," Dub said. "That little pecker-wood was highgradin' Lomax sure as hell. He was taking that ore to Salt Lake at night. Lomax caught him at it and Sonny killed him. I don't know how he did it but I'll bet you my house and barn he did."

David and Fuller exchanged glances. David wished now that he hadn't gotten involved. That he hadn't been so impulsive. Following Sonny had been a mistake and he could tell from Fuller's expression that he thought so too.

"You boys should tell the sheriff," Dub insisted, his head bobbing, "about following Sonny. That's evidence."

"I suppose we should," David said. "I wish I had thought to notice whether or not that truck was loaded."

"We"ll just tell him what we know," Fuller said.

"Come on, I'll go with you ," Dub said, still energized by the excitement.

With Dub leading the way the three men left and walked the two blocks to Sheriff Gibson's house. The Sheriff's blue Bronco was parked in the driveway. Lights were on inside the house but no one answered when Dub knocked. They waited uneasily as Dub knocked again. In a few seconds Sheriff Gibson, a napkin in his hand, appeared at the oval glass and opened the door.

"Evening Dub," the sheriff said through the screen door. He nodded to David and Fuller.

"You having supper?" Dub said.

"Just finished," Gibson said.

"Well, I hate to bother you," Dub said, animated, "but Doc here has something to tell you that we think you ought to know. About Sonny Lott."

The sheriff, concerned, looked at David, turned the latch on the screen and opened the door. "Come on in."

21 ✝✝✝✝

David turned the bone over and ran his finger down the shaft. The grain was rough and raised like an old barn board.

"As you can see," Professor Cowan said, pointing with a pencil, "these linear scrape marks stand out quite clearly. They were made with a sharp object." David held the bone so Fuller could see. The four narrow lines, almost parallel and just lighter than the gray of the bone itself, extended nearly the length of the shaft.

"That is the left thigh bone," said Cowan, "the femur of the subject we have identified as Bell. Victim A. But all the long bones from each of the skeletons have these marks." David and Fuller studied the bone.

"You say all the bones showed these marks?" Fuller asked

"All the long bones," Cowan corrected. "Here," he said, handing a bone to Fuller. "This is the right femur from Victim E. Most probably Humphreys. The markings are here," he pointed, "and here."

"Humphreys?"

"We think so," Cowan said, looking over his glasses at Fuller. "If we have identified the victims' remains correctly, Victim B is Noon, the teenager. Victim C is Swan, the oldest. Victim D is Miller whose skull was missing, and Victim E is Humphreys, the large man with the heavy muscle attachments on the bones. Victim A, therefore, is Bell.

"Impressive," said David.

"It appears," Cowan said, "there was rather extensive defleshing of each of the victim's bodies."

"Could these marks have been made by animals?" Fuller asked.

"It's very unlikely," replied Cowan. "The gnawing marks made by animal teeth are more numerous and shorter, and are not all oriented along the length of the bone as these are. Also, animals don't tend to deflesh the bones at the site but rather disarticulate the bones at the joints and carry the limbs away to eat elsewhere. The fact that these skeletons were intact suggests that the bodies were not eaten by animals." Cowan paused. "And that's strange, too, isn't it," he mused. "You would expect some animal scavenging. It's as if the bodies were . . . attended."

"As if Hammit were near-by?" Fuller suggested.

"Perhaps," Cowan nodded.

"So," said David, "from what you can tell it seems pretty clear there was cannibalism."

"Almost certainly," Cowan said.

"And fairly systematic," Fuller suggested. "All victims. All long bones. Either Hammit cooly harvested all the flesh at the time of the murders or he kept coming back."

"Would flesh have spoiled faster after it was cut from the bone?" David asked.

"It probably wouldn't have made much difference," Cowan said. "Nighttime temperatures in March at that altitude would have been cold enough to freeze the flesh—on the bodies or off—and keep it frozen during the day. Especially if the bodies were shaded or covered with snow."

David and Fuller handed the bones back. Cowan placed them on the desk behind him.

"The skulls were quite interesting, as well" Cowan said. He took a skull from the desk and turning, held it out to David and Fuller. The vault of the skull was cracked in two places and a piece was broken away completely

"You are familiar with this, Dr. Walton," Cowan said pointing with the pencil. "There is some separation of the skull bones here along these wavy suture lines. That is natural as the bones dry and shrink. But here," he said holding the loose piece of skull bone in place, "these marks, these angular fractures, these were made by a sharp object long enough to make a cut this length, and heavy enough—or moving fast enough—to fracture bone."

"Like a hatchet?" David suggested.

"Like a hatchet," Cowan said over his glasses.

"Why couldn't these fractures have been produced by the weight of the rock and dirt in the grave," Fuller asked.

Cowan put the skull down on the table and held up the triangular piece of bone that had been broken away. "The bone of the skull," he began with a classroom tone, "is like a sandwich. There is a thin outer table of cortical bone here," he pointed to the broken edge, "and a thin inner table of cortical bone here. Between these two is a honeycomb layer of lighter medullary bone. Together these layers give the skull strength without the heavy weight of solid bone."

Fuller was looking closely.

Cowan continued. "When the skull is fractured from the outside by a high velocity blow such as a bullet or a sharp object, where the force is concentrated in a small area, the bone of the inner table is broken away farther back from the fracture line than the bone of the outer table so the broken edge is not square but beveled at an angle. Like knapped flint. Like this." He held the bone fragment to reveal the broken edge and then handed it to Fuller.

"An exit wound, on the other hand, bevels the outer table."

"So this beveling suggests that this skull was fractured by a blow with a sharp object," Fuller said.

"A sharp object moving with great velocity," Cowan confirmed.

Fuller inspected the fragment then handed it to David who examined at it and returned it to Cowan.

"Each of the four skulls we examined—one was missing you will recall—had several of these characteristic fractures."

For a moment Cowan's explanation was lost on David. Then with surprised realization, he said, "All the skulls had several fractures? Even Bell's?"

"Yes," said Cowan with a slow nod. "Even Bell's. We think this is Bell's skull."

"But," David paused, thinking, "I had the impression from what Hammit said that he only hit Bell once with the hatchet. To finish him off after he shot him." David looked to Fuller for confirmation.

"But Hammit never actually said he only hit Bell once," Fuller said.

"Well . . . ." David began.

"Hammit's testimony may not be reliable on that account," Cowan suggested. "Even if it happened as Hammit said, he was killing a man who was trying to kill him. Terrified and enraged, he might easily have struck Bell more than once."

"I suppose you're right, "David agreed.

Fuller bent to look closely at the skull on the desk. "There is no bullet wound in Bell's skull," Fuller said pointing over the left eye socket.

"No," said Cowan.

David recalled that Fuller had pointed out how Hammit, when questioned at the second trial, had said he shot Bell in the forehead, contradicting his statement at the first trial when he said he shot Bell through the belly. The look Fuller and David exchanged recalled that discussion.

"So," said Fuller, pausing, "there were multiple fractures, presumably from an object like a hatchet in all the skulls."

"That's correct," said Cowan.

Fuller turned to David and smiled mischievously. "Hammit killed them all in their sleep, didn't he?"

"Well, now . . . ," David protested.

"I'm not sure I would say that," Cowan said thoughtfully. "But what we have found is compatible with that suggestion. Here is some other evidence that will interest you."

Cowan took another bone from the table. "This is a forearm bone. The right forearm, the ulna in this case. This particular specimen is also from victim A."

"Bell?" David asked.

"Yes," Cowan said, holding the bone to the light. "Can you see these little wedge-shaped nicks here along the free edge.

David and Fuller leaned closer.

"These are what we call parre, or defense marks," Cowan said. "When a person is attacked he instinctively raises one or both of his arms in defense and crosses them in front of his face to ward off the blow. Like this." Cowan demonstrated. Then pointing to the shaft of the bone, "This narrow edge of the bone is then toward the attacker. If some of the blows are taken on this forearm raised for protection and if the blows are made with a sharp object, the edge of the bone can actually be cut. Here." He pointed to three small nicks.

"You said this bone was from Bell's forearm?" Fuller asked.

"If we have identified the skeletons correctly," Cowan replied.

"But," David said, troubled. "Hammit only hit Bell in the head."

"Or did he?" challenged Fuller. "First, Hammit said he shot Bell in the belly. Then he said he shot him in the head. He said he hit Bell only to finish him off but there are multiple hatchet wounds in his skull, too. Now it looks as if he bludgeoned Bell to death, maybe even in his blankets. Like the others. I mean, if these marks were made as Professor Cowan suggests, it means Bell died defending himself from a series of blows."

David turned to Cowan. "How sure are you that this bone belongs to Bell?"

"Well," said Cowan, who had been listening to the exchange, "in this case, gentlemen, it doesn't make any difference."

"No difference?" David said with polite disbelief. "But . . . ."

"No," said Fuller who had now caught on. He held out his hand to interrupt David. "All the victims had these marks on their forearms." He turned to Cowan. "Didn't they?"

"Every one, "Cowan confirmed.

"All of them?" David said.

Cowan nodded.

"So," said Fuller, "all the skulls had multiple hatchet wounds, and all the forearms showed evidence that each man had died trying to defend himself."

"Yes," Cowan said.

"Pretty convincing," Fuller said to David.

"Well," David began reluctantly, "what about the gunshot wound. Did you find any evidence that would confirm Bell had been shot?"

"We x-rayed all the bones," Cowan said. "There were no traces of lead on any of the bones." David looked resigned. "But," Cowan continued, "that doesn't mean, of course, that Bell was not shot. Only that the bullet—if there was one—struck no bones. It is difficult to prove the absence of something.

David sat thinking.

"How would you put this together? "Fuller asked Cowan.

"Well," replied Cowan folding his arms and leaning back on the front of the desk, "all five men appear to have died violently, most likely as a result of head trauma. They each appear to have been conscious during at least part of the attack, but unable—perhaps too weak—to defend themselves successfully. And," he paused, "there is considerable evidence to support cannibalism."

David and Fuller sat pondering this information. Professor Cowan broke the silence.

"I'm afraid it doesn't actually settle anything, does it. Unfortunately, that is often the case."

"Well," said Fuller, "it does raise some questions about how Bell died and whether or not Hammit was telling the truth about that.

"Did you find anything else?" asked Fuller.

"No. I've told you everything." Cowan took off his glasses and let them hang from the cord around his neck. "I'll prepare a written report, of course. You will want that."

"Yes," said David.

"And the bones . . .?" Cowan said, nodding toward the five cardboard boxes on the floor beside the desk. "Will you be taking them with you today, or . . . ."

"Oh. Yes," said David looking at Fuller who agreed. "We should do that."

"I'll just put these with the others," the professor said. He took the bones from the desk top and placed them, one at a time, in the cartons and folded down the lids. "There," he said straightening up.

"You have been very helpful, Professor Cowan."

"Yes," Fuller added.

"Well, gentlemen, I have certainly enjoyed our little project and I want to thank you on behalf of the students. This has been a very instructive exercise for them."

The three men shook hands.

"I'll have the cartons brought down for you," Cowan said. "Is your car parked nearby?"

"Yes," said. "In the visitor's lot.

"Good," said Cowan as they walked together toward the door of his office. "Pull around to the front of the building. The cartons will be there in five minutes."

*   *   *

"Well," David said to Fuller as they sat in the car. "What do you think now?"

"I think it's over. The bones didn't settle it and there are no more leads to run down. No more clues. No more experts to talk to."

"And no answers," David said flatly.

"And no answers," Fuller repeated. "That's the worst part, isn't it?"

"In a way," David said. "But maybe the worst part is that the hunt is over. I was enjoying it." He leaned forward and started the car. "What time is it?

"Four-thirty."

"You want to drive back to Henson tonight?"

"May as well," Fuller said. Got to get these guys back." He jerked his thumb over his shoulder at the five cartons in the trunk.

David headed north on 285 into the warm technicolor of the afternoon. The low sun brightened the clumps of bunch grass and made long blue shadows behind the juniper bushes. Saffron chamisa and the last of the blue asters bloomed in the ditches beside the road and in the deeper creases of the wrinkled land, the gold-green-gold foliage of the cottonwoods glowed as if lit from within. On the mountains behind town aspen groves filled the cirques and bowls near timberline like bright yellow glaciers.

At Espanola they turned west and crossed the river. As he reached the other side, David suddenly pulled over onto the dirt shoulder and stopped the car.

Fuller, surprised, turned to David for an explanation.

"I know what happened!" He blurted out, hands still gripping the wheel. "I should have thought of it before!" He turned to face Fuller. "Look. Suppose Hammit did kill the others. How could he have done that? How could one man weakened by hunger and the cold overpower five men? Even if they were sleeping? Surely the struggle would have aroused them to defend themselves. I mean, how quick can you kill five men with a hatchet?"

"Well, the marks on their arm bones suggested they were defending themselves."

"But they couldn't! That's just it. They were awake and trying to defend themselves but they couldn't. How come Hammit had the strength to kill five men with a hatchet and none of the five had the strength to protect himself?" David asked rhetorically.

Fuller was trying to follow him.

"Hammit poisoned them!" David said, convinced. "With the bromides!"

"Bromides?"

"Right. Bromide was the standard treatment for epilepsy in those days. Bromide is a sedative. A central nervous system depressant. It calms the hyperexcitability of the epileptic's nervous system and prevents irritable focus in the brain from setting off the seizures."

"But he, or someone, bashed their heads in," Fuller protested.

"I don't mean the bromide killed them. A dose large enough to kill them would have made them vomit it all up. But in smaller doses, bromide is a sedative. It causes somnolence and drowsiness. Hammit would have known that from the side effects he must have had."

"So, he drugged them and in that state they were unable to resist his attacks."

"Exactly!"

"But . . . ."

"It's perfect!"

"But, if he ate the bodies afterward, wouldn't he have been poisoned too?"

"One gram of bromide would have been more than enough to sedate each man. Even ten times that amount distributed throughout the body of a hundred-and fifty pound man wouldn't have left a toxic concentration in the muscles. Even if Hammit ate . . ."

"I get the picture," Fuller said with disgust.

"Almost certainly, Hammit was taking bromides. Probably that was his medicine box McNutt found at the campsite."

"Then how come he still had seizures? McGrue and Pounds both said Hammit had them on the trip from Utah."

"Well, it wasn't perfect but it was the only treatment they had then. And there's another interesting thing. One of the side effects of chronic bromide treatment was mania or psychotic behavior. Many patients suffering from bromism were often committed to mental institutions."

"Maybe that's why people thought Hammit was so strange?"

" . . . and explains his inappropriate behavior at his trial," David added.

Fuller sat back in his seat, thinking. "You know, Walton, maybe you're onto something."

"Proving it is the problem though, isn't it."

"Could Cowan help?"

"Maybe. Some toxins are concentrated in bone. He didn't mention the results of any toxin screens on the bones, did he."

"I can't believe he would overlook that."

"Maybe not. But it's going to be easy to find out, isn't it?"

22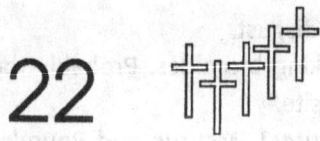

Sunset and evening bell . . . and one clear call for me . . . and
may there be no moaning of the bar . . . when I put out to sea . . .

Gathered in the narrow geology of the valley, ringed around the six white posts of the grave site, thirty people stood in respectful mufti singing the hymn chosen by the minister. All day long it had been trying to rain. Now the gray sky lay softly on the peaks, roofing over the rocky nave and transept of the valley like a flannel tent, sound-proofing it, and into that soft silence the simple harmony of the thin, earnest voices rose and disappeared.

Sunset and evening bell . . . and after that the dark
and may there be no sadness of farewell . . . when I,
when I embark . . .

Jolene Ponder had worked for a week organizing the burial ceremony. It was her idea to have the services at sunset. She said it was befitting death. The Presbyterian minister spoke as he said he would, and as he agreed was brief. The flowers, five single red roses, one on each low dirt mound, were selected for their symbolism and their simplicity.

For such a tide as moving seems asleep . . . too full for
sound or foam . . . when that drew from out the
boundless deep . . . turns again home . . . turns home.

For though from out our bourne of time and place
the flood may bear me far . . . I hope to see my pilot
face to face . . . when I have crossed the bar.

The singing stopped. There was a moment of uneasy silence attending the uncertainty. Mrs. Ponder stepped forward.

"Thank you all for coming," she said turning to look at the circle of faces. Then, checking silently with the minister who nodded, she said, "That concludes the program."

Duty done, the singers, as if needed elsewhere, turned up their collars against the gray chill and with soft words and nods to Mrs. Ponder excused themselves and made their way down the hill to their cars.

"That was very nice," David said walking over and taking her hand.

"I think it went off all right, don't you?" she said to David, hopefully .

"It was perfect," he reassured her.

"Well," she paused, "it was the least we could do. I feel so sorry for those men. They were so far from home. Some of them just boys."

"Well," said David, "it was a very nice thing for you to do."

She smiled bravely and taking Dub's arm followed the others. David and Fuller stayed in what was left of the day and watched the lights of the little caravan as it wound its way down the valley towards town and out of sight.

David walked over to the railing and the six white posts and stood looking down at the graves. Then turning to Fuller, "Do you feel like you knew these men or am I just being sentimental again?" Fuller didn't answer but walked over beside him.

David squatted down and picked up a handful of granular dirt and let it sift through his fingers. "What do you figure," he said, "it must have been about the first week of March when they died here?"

"If Hammit was right about the number of days they spent traveling from Ouray's camp. Why?"

"I was just thinking. Early March, 1874. What was going on in the world in March of 1874?"

"It was the Opulent Era," Fuller answered. "Victoria, the Empress of India, was Queen of England. Dickens' Christmas Carol was a best seller. Ulysses Grant was just starting his second term. In the salons of Europe and the east coast, couples waltzed to Strauss, and people were being shocked by Impressionists' paintings and Wagner's operas."

"It's ironic, isn't it? These guys were out here in the wilderness struggling with the most basic elements of survival while in Paris and Philadelphia men their same age danced at balls with lace handkerchiefs tucked up their sleeves."

"You never know where your choices will take you, do you?"

"We learned to fear the places that we went, least the sender, unaware, deceive the sent."

"Who said that?" Fuller asked.

"I did," replied David with a smile.

*   *   *

The pinon logs snapped in the fireplace and filled the small cabin with their woody incense. David poured a cup of coffee from the blue and white speckled coffee pot and after offering it silently to Fuller returned it to the stone hearth. He crossed the room, sat down heavily next to his friend and propped his feet on the low table in front of the sofa.

"You really thought the bones were going to show traces of bromide, didn't you ?"

"You know," David said nodding, "I really did. It seemed like such a good idea. But mind you, he still could have poisoned them. It's only because bromide isn't concentrated in bone that I can't prove it." Then turning so he could look Fuller in the face he said, "Be honest. You thought there'd be bromide in those bones too, didn't you?"

"Yeah," Fuller admitted. "I did. I must say you had me convinced. Now I'm not so sure."

"Not so sure he poisoned them?"

"Not so sure that he killed them. I was actually expecting Bell's skeleton to show evidence of a bullet wound."

"That doesn't mean he didn't shoot Bell. I mean, if he shot him through the belly, the bullet might easily have missed any bony structures. And besides, even if we knew he shot Bell, that doesn't mean he didn't kill the others."

"Maybe so. But if Hammit didn't kill them, he sure paid a hell-of-a price for having a bad reputation."

From the bedroom, the telephone rang insistently. David went out to answer it and was gone for several minutes. He returned smiling.

"Who was that?" Fuller asked as David sat down beside him.

"Sheriff Gibson."

"What's so funny?"

"It's not funny, really. It's just ironic. They arrested Sonny Lott this morning."

"Where?"

"In Wyoming."

"You're kidding."

"That's what he said. Apparently, he's already confessed. David paused. "He said he killed Lomax in self-defense."

"Self-defense!" Fuller said, incredulous.

"He said Lomax tried to run him over and he shot him."

Fuller looked at David, furrowed his brow and then began to smile. He put his coffee cup on the table, leaned back in the sofa and locked his fingers behind his head.

"Bro-ther," he said. "That's too much."

"You don't suppose Lott's telling the truth, do you?" David said with a mischievous smile.

Fuller raised his head just enough to give David a skeptical glance, then leaned back and closed his eyes. "I think I'll just let that one play itself out."

www.ingramcontent.com/pod-product-compliance
Lightning Source LLC
Chambersburg PA
CBHW011506170626
46812CB00008B/2997